The Vicious Battle for the Claydoms

LOOK EAST

TIM KIRBY

LOOK EAST
Copyright © 2024 by Tim Kirby

All rights reserved. Neither this publication nor any part of this publication may be reproduced or transmitted in any form or by any means, electronic or mechanical, including photocopying, recording or any information storage and retrieval system, without permission in writing from the author.

This is a work of fiction. Names, characters, places and incidents either are the product of the author's imagination or are used fictitiously, and any resemblance to actual persons, living or dead, businesses, companies, events, or locales is entirely coincidental.

Printed in Canada

ISBN: 978-1-4866-2573-4
eBook ISBN: 978-1-4866-2574-1

Word Alive Press
119 De Baets Street Winnipeg, MB R2J 3R9
www.wordalivepress.ca

WORD ALIVE
—P R E S S—

MIX
Paper | Supporting responsible forestry
FSC® C103567

Cataloguing in Publication information can be obtained from Library and Archives Canada.

To all who search for Truth and Justice.

For if at the breaking of the day you look intently towards the east, and if you comprehend in the fading grey of the waning darkness a threatening black cloud slowly oozing into the brightening sky of Dominion, you will know it is the egocentric Powerful Darkness that abides its time, desiring to ultimately destroy Chief Adon Olam, Dominion, and what Dominion stands for, even to the destruction of Claydonia and the Claydoms.

Early Morning Encounter

The beautiful golden sunrise broke in the east as Chief Adon Olam, commander in chief of Dominion and commander of the First Dominion Headquarters Division, strolled peacefully beside the river that wound its way through the majestic parklands. Along the way, he paused to smell flowers, listen to birds, and watch wildlife. As the day warmed, a slight breeze teased the grass and rustled the dew-laden trees, causing droplets of water to fall to the moss-covered earth.

Olam was short, muscular, and dark-haired with a well-trimmed beard. Although he wasn't handsome, he had a weathered complexion and dark, smiling eyes. He walked with a slight limp, rugged and sure of himself and everything he did. He was a wise man, honest and just in his dealings with his troops. He also had a pleasant sense of humour.

Along another stretch of the same path walked General Cypher, commander of the Second Dominion Division. Cypher saw himself as handsome, brilliant, resourceful, and well-educated. A shining light to all. He was more forceful than the other generals in executing his duties, and this morning he was in a hurry. He was preoccupied with thoughts on the monthly meeting of generals.

At a sharp outcropping of willow along the banks of the river, Cypher suddenly realized he wasn't alone. He spun around to see Olam nearby.

The chief quietly smiled. "Good morning, Cypher. It's good to meet you on such a beautiful morning."

Flustered, Cypher took a few moments to focus himself. "Chief Olam! You startled me."

"What could be so important that you'd be so completely distracted from all this immense beauty?"

"With all due respect, sir, you know about the meeting of the generals," Cypher said, being blunt. "I must be prepared for it."

"Yes, but that's an hour from now."

Cypher's face clouded over with anger. "Again, with all due respect, sir, I must be ready."

"Why the urgency, Cypher?"

Without replying, Cypher turned and left in order to conceal his burning dislike for the chief.

Olam walked silently as he approached the headquarters. He pondered the reasons why Cypher was behaving so anxiously and secretively.

Upon arriving at the front doors, he encountered General Cha'el, commander of the Third Dominion Division, and General Stren, commander of the Fourth Dominion Division. He greeted them warmly.

Cha'el offered a salute. "Good morning, sir."

Stren cheerfully mentioned that he was ready for the upcoming generals meeting, as well as anything the day might bring.

Rising Tension

As soon as Cypher left Olam by the river, he rushed ahead to get inside the building first. He managed to arrive before the others and grab a cup of coffee from the lunchroom. He placed a cinnamon bun on a small plate, then made his way to the conference room.

He deposited the plate next to his usual spot at the table, just left of Olam's seat. But he didn't sit. Instead he took his coffee, walked to the far side of the room, and waited nervously. He sipped and glanced in disgust at the doors where the others would soon enter.

The next person to enter was Stren, young and robust with flowing red hair and a willing smile. He was energetic and alert, eager to achieve anything Chief Olam assigned for his division to do.

As Stren stepped inside, Cypher noticed that he was holding a plate with two cinnamon buns.

"That's awfully greedy, taking half the cinnamon buns for yourself," Cypher growled.

Stren ignored the comment and walked over to his own seat. "Good morning, General Cypher. You're still as happy and cheerful as ever."

"And you're just a devious brat," Cypher snarled. "You've never seen a real battle in your life. How'd you get your general's rank? What'd you pay for it? Did you cheat on your qualification exams, kid?"

"Cypher, it's such a bright and cheerful day. Why choose to be so miserable?"

Cypher straightened, ready to give Stren a heated lecture on military prowess when the door opened and Olam walked in alongside Cha'el and Chief Warrant Officer Hagans. Each placed their snacks on the table.

"Gentlemen, please be seated," said Olam. "It's a beautiful day here in Dominion. We have many troops at our command and a magnificent land to protect. Remember, our purpose as commanders of Dominion is to do our best for others, no matter the personal cost."

As everyone settled in, Olam called the meeting to order. It began at 0800 sharp, with Hagans noting the time and generals in attendance.

The monthly reports began with Cypher's, who smirked to himself. "All is well with my troops. As agreed, they're diligently defending Dominion." He gave them a piercing glare as he leaned back in his chair and took a bite of his cinnamon bun.

"General Cypher, is this your full report as commander of one-quarter of Dominion troops?" Olam questioned.

Deliberately ignoring the commander-in-chief, Cypher looked down at the floor and coughed. "Yes, sir!"

In the ensuing silence, Olam waited.

Cypher had to control his rising anger. He abruptly lowered his coffee cup onto the table and folded his arms, tight-lipped.

Olam looked away. "General Cha'el, would you report on the Third Division?"

"It's been a good month, with our troops looking at our training procedures," said Cha'el. "They've brought forward some excellent suggestions, changes that make it more efficient to relay information to troops on the ground. The troops' morale is high. Being part of this division is exciting and gratifying."

"Thank you, General Cha'el," Olam said. "I look forward to these changes being implemented. And it's good that morale is high." He turned to the next general around the table. "General Stren, how are things in the Fourth Division?"

"First, let me agree with General Cha'el. We've made similar changes and seen immense improvements in our troops' ability to coordinate with the joint taskforce and support units. Our last mission was highly successful in dealing with the threat and the troops returned feeling accomplished."

"Thank you, General Stren. Well done." Olam cleared his throat. "We have many things to accomplish today. Before we dismiss, I'd like to review our training mandate. First and foremost, all members of Dominion are part of our forces and are led by leaders who have proven their loyalty, honesty, and trustworthiness to Dominion. Also, our protocol is that all leaders care for those in their command. In training, every commanding officer is free to choose to do their best for their troops, no matter what it costs them. This also pertains to the headquarters division, a joint operation for land, sea, and air forces."

He paused for a moment, deciding to say no more. And with that, Olam ended the meeting.

"Thank you for your reports," he said in conclusion. "Dismissed."

Troubling Thoughts

Leaving his dishes, Cypher quickly left and rushed east to his own Second Division headquarters. Olam and Hagans brought all the dishes to the lunchroom and then disappeared into their offices.

This left Cha'el and Stren behind to consider their thoughts about Cypher.

"Cypher just insulted our chief," Stren said, frowning. "I don't like it."

"This is Cypher's true nature," Cha'el replied. "He and his division won't defend Chief Olam, nor what Dominion stands for."

"And yet Olam just reminded us that he wants us to train our troops to do the best for others, no matter the cost."

Cha'el nodded. "And considering what Dominion stands for, we have had a lasting peace for many generations. But I'm sure there'll be other revelations of Cypher's nature in the coming weeks." He stood up. "Stren, keep an eye open and listen for anything coming from Cypher and his division."

With that, Stren left the room, planning to return to his troops as soon as possible.

Cha'el decided to do the same, but as he passed Olam's office the chief called to him.

"Yes, sir?" Cha'el said, looking inside.

"Come, have a seat." Olam watched as the general sat down. "Cha'el, I have great confidence and respect for you and Stren. Yet we're having difficulties with Cypher. What's your impression of Cypher's conduct this morning?"

"Sir, Cypher is going to do what he'll do. And I appreciate your briefing of the training protocol. I know you were sending Cypher a message, reminding him that the First, Third, and Fourth Divisions will support you. If he's planning anything, we'll stand together to defend Dominion and everything Dominion stands for."

"Thanks, Cha'el. I knew you'd see the implications of my remark."

And yet Olam remained troubled. No doubt there would soon be a threat rising in the east.

Inside Second Division

With flashing eyes and clenched fists, Cypher madly kicked rocks on his way towards Second Division's headquarters. He felt a surge of rage towards Olam.

"I'll kill that good for nothing filthy pig," he growled to himself as he reached for the front door's handle. "That arrogant filthy sewer rat…"

As soon as he entered, he turned on his chief administrator.

"Get me a coffee! Now!"

Within moments, he had walked into his own office and slammed the door behind him. He found that he wasn't alone. Sitting in the corner was his special agent, none other than In'Mutin.

"In'Mutin, the faster I get rid of that good-for-nothing lying, stealing, cheating neurotic sociopath, the better I'd like it!" He roared.

"Settle down and listen to me," In'Mutin soothed. "I'm your best friend. We've planned this overthrow for months, so control yourself. Don't expose everything we've planned by acting like this. I know that you want to take Dominion and replace Olam as commander-in-chief. I know you're the ultimate leader. Just because you see yourself as the bright star doesn't mean you can act like this. You'll blow the takeover."

But Cypher was in no mood for the agent's reassurances or advice.

"No, you listen to me." Cypher, poking his chest declared, "I earned my rights and freedoms as commander of Second Division. My duty is to protect Dominion's rights and freedoms from Olam's selfish oppression. Yes, I'm the mightiest warrior of Dominion and should be commander-in-chief. Olam stole that role from me. And mark my words, In'Mutin, I'll eliminate you or anyone who doesn't do what's ordered to destroy Olam and everything he stands for. You know full well that I put Captain Cur'sent in command of our first company. He's brilliant. He'll be central to my plans."

"Cypher, I'm the one who suggested you put him in that position."

"But I'm the one who gave him all the authority and power he needs to follow my orders."

Just then, a knock sounded on the door.

"Come in!" Cypher shouted in disgust.

When the door opened, his administrator entered slowly, carrying two cup of coffees and a cinnamon roll for each of them. She placed them on Cypher's desk.

"It's about time." Cypher couldn't help being impatient. "Close the door behind you."

In'Mutin picked up the cinnamon role and took a bite. "Thank you! I didn't think I'd get a snack this morning."

The administrator quietly closed the door and left them feeling the tension.

When they were alone again, Cypher grabbed what would turn out to be his second cinnamon roll of the day.

"Cur'sent is second only to you," In'Mutin continued. "He's old school and demands obedience. He's well-known and highly praised for his military prowess. I've seen how much the troops under his command respect him."

"He's ruthless," Cypher agreed. "You'll also recall that I installed Captain Cardinal as commanding officer of the second company. I chose her because she's gorgeous and skilled in persuasion. She knows what she wants and has the ability to get it."

"Again, you chose her at my prompting."

"It's always your suggestion…"

In'Mutin shook his head. "Her natural talent brought her to our attention. Everyone wants to be as persuasive as she is. Have you noticed that the troops practically worship her?"

"I didn't only choose her at your suggestion, In'Mutin. I chose her because, like Cur'sent, she comes from the far edges of Dominion. In fact, I chose both because they'll be powerful officers under my command."

In truth, both Cur'sent and Cardinal were so attractive that he expected the troops would easily submit to their ways.

"Given our intelligence and wit, that filthy Olam doesn't stand a chance," said In'Mutin.

"In'Mutin, what are you doing today?" Cypher suddenly demanded.

"If you haven't another assignment for me, I'll monitor Olam, Cha'el, and Stren to see what I can pick up."

"Good! I want to know exactly what they're doing. I need to get the jump on them."

Guarded Decisions

Olam looked east out his office window, gazing at the Second Division headquarters off in the distance. Turning to Cha'el, he continued.

"You and I both know Cypher is planning an uprising," Olam murmured. "This morning, Cypher deliberately gave an inadequate report of his division's activities. It reveals his burning anger towards me."

Cha'el continued, "I've seen Cypher's egocentric nature in the work we've done together. I have a feeling he's convincing his troops that he'll be their liberator. Their way out of Dominion. No doubt he's encouraging their selfishness as a way of getting what he wants. But his troops don't understand that he's only using them."

"I agree." Olam turned to his guest. "Have you and Stren noticed any increase in troop transfers between the various divisions?"

"Yes, many have transferred to the Second from the Third and Fourth. I'm certain they're transferring in order to join the uprising. I'd say those transfers are encouraging Cypher to push ahead more quickly." Cha'el cleared his throat. "And yet there are also disgruntled troops who are transferring out of the Second. Many don't even know there's a rebellion in the works. They're just trying to separate themselves from toxic leadership."

Olam gave him a nod. "Thanks for your insight. Watch these troops from the Second Division, since some may be trying to spy on us. Even so, I know that First Division is secure. Its troops are dedicated to Dominion."

The chief let out a long sigh as he turned and looked back through the window.

"Cha'el, we're in for troubling times," Olam said. "Before the peace is shattered, I'd like you to know that I appreciate your loyalty and dedication. I respect your leadership and am pleased that you've gotten to know each of your troops by name. I've also notice that your troops are content and confident. With this darkness descending on us from the east, I know I can count on your support."

Cha'el flushed with satisfaction in a job well done. "Thank you, Chief. I too appreciate your leadership and support. You can be confident that I'll support you and Dominion, as I always have."

"Thank you, General. Next week is our monthly parade and day of celebration. It will be an opportunity to celebrate Dominion before this darkness descends on us."

Cha'el nodded and then left the chief's office.

A few minutes later, Olam watched as Cha'el departed through the front doors of the building, directly below his window. The general donned his cap and took a moment to look east toward Second Division headquarters. But instead of walking in that direction, he turned north to approach the Third Division offices, no doubt intent on discussing the situation with his friend, General Stren.

Olam got up and left the office to fetch himself a cup of tea, all the while pondering a new covert operation that would serve to protect Dominion. And there was only one man to lead this operation: Chief Warrant Officer Hagans.

"Rebecca, would you please ask Hagans to come to my office?" he said to his office administrator as he closed the door behind him.

"Yes, sir!" she said cheerily.

Only minutes later, Rebecca returned with Hagans in tow.

"Thanks for coming, Hagans. Please be seated," Olam said as the chief warrant officer came in and closed the door behind him. "Because of the consequences of the current situation, I have to insist that what we're about to discuss be held in the strictest confidence."

"Yes, sir."

"As you may know, Cypher has decided to rebel against Dominion."

"Yes, sir. His troops are actively spying on your whereabouts, gathering intelligence on all your dealing. I've been hard at work to ensure those spies deliver only one report back to him: 'All is well in Dominion.'"

Olam appreciated the officer's initiative. "Very good. And let's continue all our regular interdivision communications. There must be no indication that we even suspect what he's up to. Knowing Cypher, he's keeping very alert."

"Chief, I have another suggestion. We should step up references to defence planning in our monthly directives to all generals and staff. It will keep Cypher off-balance."

Olam found himself looking east out the window again. As he did, a white-breasted nuthatch flew onto a branch of a nearby tree. It flitted up and down the trunk in search of food.

"Yes," Olam said thoughtfully. "Let's call our covert operation 'Operation Nuthatch'. And I would like you to lead it, with Cha'el and Stren. The first objective will be to change Dominion's strategic defence plan to an internal protocol."

"I'll get to work on this immediately, since we don't know Cypher's timeline," Hagan said.

"I want you to be my main contact. Cha'el and Stren shouldn't deviate from their usual comings and goings from headquarters."

"Chief, I agree. I also advise that we continue with the parade and celebration day as if there's no threat to Dominion. It may give us time to learn more about what Cypher's planning."

"Yes, very good. Let's wait and see."

Olam looked away from the window. He had now had briefings with both Cha'el and Hagans. He also felt the need to speak with Stren, but he wanted to do it without Cypher knowing. Cypher no doubt had troops watching each of the generals.

"What would be the least conspicuous way to meet with Stren?" Olam asked after a few moments of careful thought.

"Is there a way you can arrange to run into him on your early morning walk?"

Olam brightened. "Yes, I could do that. Inform Stren to meet on the path near the river, where the willows grow in a large cluster. I'll wait a bit east of the point where the path divides into two. While I meet Stren on the north path, perhaps Cha'el can take the south path, to distract anyone who may be keeping watch."

"The meeting would be brief, by necessity. But it would have to happen soon."

"Yes, sir," said Hagans. "I'll take care of it."

"Thank you, Hagans. I know this is the beginning of a long, drawn-out process. Let's do our best for Dominion." Olam managed a slight smile. "Operation Nuthatch has begun."

Once he was left alone, Olam leaned forward on his desk. He would have to allow for events to unfold as they would. If he acted too quickly, he would tip his hand and give the traitor an advantage.

Covert Rendezvous

On Monday morning, Olam walked east along the designated path, taking in the beauty and silence, knowing this could change in a moment. Coming to the fork in the trail at the willows, he glanced around and quickly stepped out of sight.

He waited for the sound of the two generals approaching. After some time, Stren descended a slight decline to the north and Cha'el disappeared down the south path.

Olam caught Stren's attention as they crossed to the river's edge. "Stren."

"Yes, sir."

"This must be quick. You and Cha'el both realize that Cypher is planning a revolt very shortly."

"Yes, sir."

"As chief, I'm asking you to be courageous. Do not be frightened in the face of a mighty and ferocious battle. Stren, hear me well: we'll overcome this darkness and again be the peaceful and beautiful Dominion we know today. In this battle, we'll all be tested, and I know you'll stand worthy of your position."

The general took this in without a word.

"Let Cha'el know I'd like each of you to contact Hagans tomorrow morning. Come to him as if you're seeking information from a clerk. Hagans will fill you in on our plans. The codename is Operation Nuthatch."

Lastly, he instructed Stren to continue along the path and meet Cha'el at the east fork.

"Be strong, my faithful friend," Olam finished.

Stren turned to him one last time. "Thank you, sir."

Olam listened to the river, giving Stren time to meet Cha'el. He then heard the rustling of willows behind him. Slowly turning, he noticed someone he hadn't seen before: a soldier with a Second Division insignia hiding in the willows. Olam smiled. The soldier didn't realize that he'd been spotted.

Slowly straightening, Olam turned towards the hiding soldier and cleared his throat. Whirling around, the soldier was shocked at having been discovered.

"Sir!" he blurted out. "I didn't expect to see you here."

"Good morning, soldier. Did you have a good walk this morning?"

"Yes, sir."

"Is there anything I could help you with?"

"No, sir. I'm waiting for some of my fellow troops."

"What's your name?"

The soldier hesitated. "I'm called Abdul." He looked uncomfortable, perhaps trying to come up with a plausible reason for being there. "I thought I'd hide and then jump out to scare them."

Olam just smiled again. "Good day, soldier. And say good morning to your friends from me."

Shaken and not knowing what to do about this encounter with Olam, the soldier remained rooted to the spot, anxiously waiting until several other soldiers from the Second Division arrived.

"That lowdown, filthy, good for nothing pig Olam discovered my hiding place," the soldier snapped, being extremely aggravated. "He scared the living daylights out of me." He turned on his comrades in anger and flew into a rage. "Why weren't you here to help take him out?"

The confrontation quickly broke into a fistfight, but eventually cooler heads prevailed and everyone calmed down.

"What will we tell our commanding officer?" the soldier wondered.

One of the others, a private, spoke next. "Here's our line... we'll tell him that we met a bear and had to fight it off!"

Still another, this one a corporal, could only laugh. "Yer stupider than our idiot commander."

This only made things worse, and soon the yelling and punching continued. Only after they'd argued for another few minutes did they finally make peace and start making their way back to the Second Division compound.

Once the soldiers had returned, they reported to their commanding officer. He was shocked at the troops' black eyes and disheveled uniforms.

"Sir, it was a vicious fight, but we finally fought the bear off," the private explained. "Being so badly wounded, we had to help each other back to base."

Their commander took this in. "Soldiers, I'm proud of your courage. Report immediately to sickbay for medical attention. Then report for light duty."

But the medic had many questions about the soldiers' strange story.

"So tell me," said the medic as he examined them. "Why don't you have bites and scratches from the bear?"

All stood silent for a time. No one had a good answer for this.

Upon leaving sickbay, they finished cleaning up their uniforms and reported for light duty as ordered.

The Promotion

Cypher's decision to pair Cur'sent and Cardinal proved to be an excellent military strategy. Through diligent training, they soon became one.

"Ya know, In'Mutin, I see the two working closely together," Cypher said to his special agent while they waited for the monthly parade to begin. "Cardinal, with her skills of persuasion, has greatly stimulated Cur'sent to action. They'll become a powerful influence on the troops, allowing me to win any conflict."

In'Mutin merely nodded as the day got underway.

The celebration was a huge success. Soldiers marched through the streets, carrying equipment and showcasing the colours of Dominion's various divisions, brigades, battalions, companies, platoons, and special operations. Each formed up according to their designated rank to be reviewed by their commander-in-chief.

Afterward Olam took the podium and spoke to the rank and file.

"I welcome all troops to our monthly parade and celebration," the chief called. "I congratulate all commanders and troops for a job well done in training, protecting, and caring for

Dominion." He then turned and introduced the officer standing on his left. "Let's now welcome General Cypher, commanding officer of the Second Division."

Cypher stepped forward. "I congratulate the Second Division on your skills in training. You'll be triumphant if deployed into the greatest battle ever fought! You're equal to any task. I know none of you will shrink from your duty, that you'll perform to your full capacity."

The crowd cheered. Cypher was delighted by the soldiers' response.

"Captains Cur'sent and Cardinal, come to the podium," he said as the forces quieted. The two captains stepped up. "I now command you to swear allegiance to myself and the Second Division."

Once he'd sworn them in to their new positions, Cypher reached out to present new insignias and medals to each one. In high fashion, he pinned these new decorations onto their uniforms.

With this solemn contract completed, Cypher took their hands and raised them high, to the cheers of all.

Once these honours had been bestowed, Olam invited the other generals to address their own troops.

After all the commendations were awarded, Olam returned to the podium.

"It's time to celebrate Dominion and everything Dominion stands for!" he shouted. "You are dismissed."

In true military fashion, it was a glorious celebration.

Uneasy Times

Two weeks after the parade, Olam called Rebecca, "Would you have Chief Warrant Officer Hagans come to my office?"

It only took a few minutes for Hagans to arrive and sit down.

"How's it going with Operation Nuthatch?" Olam asked.

"Very well, sir. We've had several meetings, upped our training, and quietly organized equipment so as not to alarm Cypher."

"Well done. We need to be fully alert, especially after what Cypher said at the parade."

"Yes, sir. I was taken aback by how the swearing-in oath was conducted. He rewrote it and changed the contract for newly commissioned officers. Instead of swearing allegiance to you as commander-in-chief, he had them swear allegiance to himself."

Olam sighed. "That disturbed me as well. There's an uneasiness building as everyone senses the coming conflict. It seems Cypher's troops are trained, ready, and willing to fight to get what they want. He seems ready to take on all of Dominion. I've tried working through the rising tensions, but he keeps rejecting my help."

"And he keeps accusing you and the other generals of meddling in his affairs."

"Let's keep going with Operation Nuthatch and keep alert to any indication that he's going to launch an attack."

As time went on, the tensions only got worse.

It wasn't long before the generals gathered for another regular meeting. Olam sat at the head of the table like usual, turning to Cypher when it was time for the reports.

"Cypher, how are things in the Second Division?" Olam inquired.

Immediately Cypher exploded. "Olam, I've told you before: don't meddle in my affairs with the Second Division." He pushed his chair back and stood. "You've been overstepping your boundaries and authority. In fact, you can't be trusted as chief. You've lost all moral authority to lead Dominion."

Due to Cypher's agitation, and his display over leaving the meeting in a rage, the others generals upped their surveillance of his activities.

One evening, Stren overheard several Second Division soldiers talking to themselves after a day of training.

"I've persuaded another six troops from the Third Division to come over when the fighting starts," one of them said.

"How'd you get them to agree?"

"If they didn't come over, I told them that I would report them to their commander for stealing rations and other gear to trade for drugs and booze."

"Did they do those things?"

"Good grief! No wonder you're not having any success in recruitment. No! And I couldn't care less. When their commander questions them, they won't admit to talking about a rebellion. He'll assume they stole something and throw them in lockup."

Falling Out

Before the next month's parade and celebration, Cypher pulled Major Fitzgerald aside.

"What do you think of Olam and his leadership?" Cypher demanded. "I'd say he's been commander-in-chief too long and is losing it. If I were commander-in-chief, I'd relax the laws so each division can do what it wants, when it wants, how it wants, wherever it wants."

The major was uncertain about this. "With all due respect, sir, there may be things we want to do—but for the best of all, we shouldn't do them."

A minute of uneasy silence passed between them.

"How's training coming with the new procedures being implemented by General Cha'el?" Fitzgerald asked.

"I'll train my troops however I want, and you can keep your filthy nose out of what I'm doing. I don't need anyone telling me what to do or how to do it. Do you hear me?" Cypher waved his hand dismissively. "You're so stupid. You don't even know that Olam's brainwashed you. He's taken you in so far that you don't know how ignorant you've become. You think you're one of Olam's elate, but you're just a filthy blot on Dominion's forces."

Cypher stomped off in a hateful rage. But before he got far, he almost ran into In'Mutin. The special agent was smiling.

"Hey Cypher, I'm still laughing at how you walked out on Olam at the last meeting of the generals," In'Mutin said. "Yer doing great."

"Thanks, In'Mutin. I've had enough of that flea-bitten Olam and his fat-headed generals and staff. They think they're the greatest. The time has come to prepare our troops for the takeover."

Motion of Treason

Sensing that the situation was getting worse, Olam once again called on Cypher to meet with him. When the general refused, Olam called Hagans back to his office.

"Hagans, we need to be poised for a surprise attack," said Olam. "Let's gather the generals."

This time when the generals met around the table, Cypher was notably absent.

"It's with a heavy heart that I've called you here today," Olam began. "Cypher will proceed shortly with a revolt. Thank you for your diligence and hard work in preparing our troops for this conflict."

Cha'el nodded to the commander-in-chief. "And thank you for your leadership. We also come to this meeting with heavy hearts, but our troops are ready." He paused for a moment, taking in the gravity of their situation. "I move that General Cypher and all who follow him be charged as conspirators bent on treason."

Before replying, Olam turned to Stren. "What are your thoughts, General?"

"I second the motion and fully back our troops in this conflict."

Olam hung his head. "With your support of this motion and my agreement to it, I declare General Cypher and the Second Division conspirators bent on treason. Generals, alert your troops that this activity saddens me but that I fully support them and know they'll do their best in the coming days. Prepare your units for immediate engagement with the Second Division. Thank you. You are dismissed."

The Revolt

When the troops were alerted about the preparation for battle, one of Cha'el's troopers ran straight over to Cypher's office at Second Division headquarters.

"I've got to see Cypher now!" he yellow as he burst through the front doors.

Cypher, hearing the commotion, came out of his office. "Soldier, don't come in here yelling—"

"Cypher, Olam is mustering his troops!"

As the soldier ran off to hide, trembling in fear, Cypher asked an assistant to call In'Mutin right away.

"We've just received word that Olam's preparing an attack," he said to the special agent. "I don't think any of those nitwits generals know that we know, which means we have the advantage of being able to launch a surprise attack."

In'Mutin nodded. "I agree... but let's wait to see what they're doing. That'll keep Olam guessing about when and where we may attack."

"Yes, we'll stall for time. I'll tell Olam that I've changed my mind, that I want to meet to work things out."

"Good move. I'll get your brass moving."

Before the agent could leave, Cypher reached out to stop him. "In'Mutin, we've still got a couple of days. Call all of our troops in from surveillance to maximize our numbers for our first deployment."

"Let's do it!"

Olam Moves First

Once Olam had received the communication from Cypher, he immediately called to speak with Hagans.

"Cypher has just sent a message saying that he wants to reconsider, this is Cypher and In'Mutin stalling for time," Olam told the chief warrant officer. "Instruct Cha'el and Strens to deploy their divisions per Operations Nuthatch at 0700 hours tomorrow. I'll deploy First Division's first and second battalions to secure our headquarters, along with all our supply depots and communication sites. Dismissed."

By 0700 the next day, Cha'el had mustered his joint taskforce units to occupy the major bridgeheads, main highways, trainlines, seaways, and airports. Stren deployed his seventh and eighth companies to strategic battle areas.

Cha'el then alerted his forces to prepare to apprehend Cypher, In'Mutin, and the other top commanders of the Second Division.

New Dominion

By pulling in all his surveillance troops, Cypher didn't have any way of knowing that Dominion's forces were in place. Instead he sat with In'Mutin in his office while their troops amassed outside.

"In'Mutin, are you ready to be part of New Dominion?" Cypher asked with a smile.

In'Mutin saluted his commander. "Yes, sir. You've always wanted to destroy Olam. Now's the time."

Hearing the crowd of soldiers outside, Cypher looked out his window and saw the troops lining up in formation in the parade square.

Cypher stepped outside onto his balcony to address them. "Attention, troops! First company, at 1800 hours you will begin our revolt against that filthy pig Olam. You'll be the first raiding parties. As you've trained for, your point of attack will be section twelve, south on the main rail line. Second company, at 2000 hours you will proceed to take area four. Third company, at 2300 hours you must take Olam's military headquarters, as planned. And fourth company, at 0200 tomorrow, you will occupy the railheads east of the airport and advance on it. All other troops, stand by for deployment as needed."

Feeling satisfied, he looked over the troops. This is what he had been waiting for.

"Now you have your orders. We will destroy that good for nothing Olam and his useless generals. We are New Dominion. Fight as you have been trained! In winning this revolt, you'll have everything you ever dreamed of. It's yours for the taking."

He saluted his troops and then returned to his office.

The Battle

Stren's joint taskforce, patrolling south along the rail line, encountered Second Division troops at 1943 hours. Cypher's first company, not having expected any opposition, was surprised. Immediately the taskforce signals officer contacted command central.

"Command, Fourth Division joint taskforce squad Red Eye has engaged Second Division troops. Coordinates 125 miles due south on the rail line. Numbers unknown. Several members downed. Vicious resistance."

The reply came quickly. "Dispatch to Red Eye. Fourth Division sixth company light artillery eight miles north, dispatched to your coordinates. Fourth Division eighth company airborne chopper dispatched to you."

Next, the officers at dispatch passed along a report to Fourth Division headquarters. "Dispatch to headquarters. Notify top brass that the Fourth Division has encountered Second Division rebels at 1943 hours. Several Fourth Division troops downed."

At headquarters, Olam was sitting alongside the chief warrant officer.

"Hagans, call the generals and their staff to report immediately," Olam instructed him.

It didn't take long for the generals to arrive.

Olam got right down to business. "Stren, how are your troops?"

"We have twenty-eight troopers down. The fight is vicious. Backup dispatched with chopper support. Unknown number of rebels. Lots of snippers and guerilla attacks. Supplies are good."

"General Cha'el?"

"As yet, the Third Division hasn't encountered any resistance. But they've been informed that the rebellion has begun and are full alert."

"First Division has been alerted to the attack and is on surveillance duty," Olam informed them. "All sickbays and hospitals have been alerted to expect incoming injuries. Body bags and equipment are being dispatched to the medic corps. Dispatch has also notified our prisoner of war facilities to prepare for incoming." He wore a grim but determined expression. "Generals, you've been training your troops for such a time as this. Be strong and courageous. You are dismissed."

Olam watches the general once again dispersed.

The commander-in-chief returned to his office and made a call. "Dispatch, send orders for an all-out deployment on Cypher's bases, including training and supply facilities. Deploy troops to secure and hold all air, sea, and land routes previously assigned to the Second Division. Keep me and the generals informed of all activities. Thank you."

The next order he gave was to dispatch First Division's special operations to immediately secure all documents related to Cypher.

The Aftermath

Just like that, the country found itself engaged in a violent civil war. In the first days of conflict, the offensives were vicious, with casualties and wounded on both sides. Some Second Division troops defected to Dominion forces, and many Third and Fourth Division troops crossed over to Cypher's side. However, the entire First Division members stood firm, defending Dominion and Chief Olam.

As the weeks passed, those looking east saw dark rolling clouds of conflict darkening the sky.

After more than two years, the major conflict ended and Olam again called a meeting of his generals.

"Thank you for meeting," he opened. "I appreciate your diligence in calming this dark rebellion."

"Chief Olam, thank you for your confidence in our forces," said Cha'el. "We appreciate that this has been difficult for us all."

"Thank you. Together we now have the task of cleaning up and rebuilding Dominion." Olam cleared his throat. "As you know, Cypher and most of his troops have been imprisoned, wounded, or killed. Our soldiers are slowly capturing those members of the resistance still remaining. Many officers of the Second Division have been wounded and admitted to military hospitals until they recover enough to stand trial. In addition, special operations has found ample evidence that Cypher's actions constitute high treason. As expected, he sees himself as commander-in-chief of Dominion, and the members of his division call him their true leader. Many documents we've recovered reveal his plans for the so-called New Dominion. I've now instructed the courts to set up a review board of military magistrates to direct the hearing and punishment of Cypher, his leaders, and his troops."

Cha'el broke in at this point. "Chief, as generals we'd like to order an evaluation of all damages and losses we've suffered due to this conflict."

"I agree. Would you also form a joint special operations group of electrical mechanical engineers to clear Dominion of any ordinance that may cause harm?"

"Yes, sir. And I'd like to mobilize support troops to rebuild our damaged infrastructure."

"We could involve all able-bodied troops by having them assist in the cleanup," added Stren.

Olam nodded. "Yes, these are good plans. And because we've lost a major part of our forces, I'll need you both, along with Hagans, to evaluate our forces and examine how best to reestablish them. I'd like to form two new divisions from what remains of First, Third, and Fourth." He let this settle in, then changed the subject. "As we plan to bring healing to Dominion, let's organize a day of celebrations with a full parade next month. Thank you. You are dismissed."

A Celebration

It was a sombre day as the able-bodied troops marched through the streets on the day of the parade, helping their wounded comrades form up. They came to attention when Chief Olam took the podium.

Gazing over his troops, Olam stood in deep thought. He was missing more than one-third of his forces.

"It's a sad day today," he began. "As we assemble, I say to each one here or in the hospital recovering that I thank you, with the deepest gratitude, for your courage and willingness to protect Dominion and everything we stand for."

A cheer rose from the troops.

"You stood firm in protecting your privilege to remain free to do your best for others, and you did it well. Thank you."

Everyone stood silent as this truth swept over them.

"Your generals have presented each of you with a badge of honour for your dedication and service. Yet your greatest reward is knowing that you are free. We will rebuild Dominion to its former greatness, and you will be pleased with what's coming for us all."

Another cheer rose up.

"Today we are honouring two of our great leaders by decorating them as generals. Major Rafal and Major Barac, please report to the podium."

The two majors received medals from Chief Warrant Officer Hagans.

"It is with pleasure that I promote each of you to generals," Olam continued. "You have exhibited true, unselfish leadership during the revolt. Thank you. General Rafal will command Fifth Division, and General Barac will lead Sixth Division."

The greatest cheer of all was heard from the troops as the two new generals saluted the commander-in-chief.

Proceedings

In consultation with Chief Magistrate Walking Eagle, Olam made the decision to assemble the review board of military magistrates, intent on studying the cases against Cypher and the other rebels. They would meet the following Wednesday at 0800 hours.

Once the board was assembled, Chief Magistrate Walking Eagle addressed them. "Over the past months, you have evaluated the materials from Cypher's Second Division headquarters. Are you ready to present your evaluation to the courts?"

"Yes, sir," replied the chairperson, Madam Ellsworth. "It should be printed within the week."

"Thank you. We'll schedule the presentation for next Friday at 1130 hours in the high court."

"Yes, sir."

Meanwhile, the nation's head physician, Dr. Cox, spoke to the chief magistrate. "Sir, I'm forwarding you a list of all the Second Division rebels who have recovered sufficiently to stand trial."

"Thank you, Doctor. Once I receive the report, we'll enter it into the court and set a date to begin proceedings."

Preliminary Hearing

Two years after the end of the rebellion, Dominion's troops were subject to a restless contentment. The case against the rebels of the uprising was finally making their way to court. After preliminary hearings were held to enter the material evidence and witnesses, the first trial began.

Chief Magistrate Walking Eagle called the court to order. "We convene today to search out the truth and intent of those who rebelled again Chief Olam and the entirety of Dominion. This court's decision will be final. Crown Prosecutor Lamonte, call your first witness."

"Thank you, your magistrate," said the prosecutor. "I call Madam Ellsworth, chairperson of the review board of military magistrates."

They all waited as Ellsworth was sworn in.

Lamonte held up a file folder for the witness to see. "Madam Ellsworth, is this the final report of the review board of military magistrates?"

"Yes."

"Thank you." The prospector turned to Walking Eagle. "Your honour, I present this report as evidence."

Once this simple business was concluded, Madam Ellsworth stepped down.

"Defence counsel Adams, do you have any witness?" asked Walking Eagle.

"Not at this time, your honour."

"Thank you." Walking Eagle looked over the court before proceeding. "As agreed by all participants, this trial will concern the senior officer in charge of deployment for the Second Division, first company commander Major Cur'sent. We'll recess until tomorrow at 0800 hours. Crown prosecutor, that will be your opportunity to present an opening statement."

With that, the preliminary hearing concluded.

The Trial

Once the court was back in session the following morning, the crown prosecutor was given his opportunity to submit an opening statement.

"There is sufficient evidence that Major Cur'sent was a key contributor to the rebellion," began Lamonte. "He fully supported General Cypher's plan to utterly annihilate Chief Olam and the other generals of Dominion. The major also helped promote Cypher as commander-in-chief, and we've found that he and Major Cardinal worked to place Cypher in control of everyone and everything in Dominion. Cur'sent has stated that it was General Cypher alone who knew best how to control his forces, and he promised that they would all be fed, housed, clothed, educated, and made healthy.

"There is also sufficient evidence that anyone who disagreed with Cypher's beliefs or ways of doing things, at any time, were either placed in workcamps or immediately executed. It was discovered in the materials seized from Second Division headquarters that Cur'sent was a key contributor to training for the rebellion. His main goal was to ensure that all Second Division soldiers were trained to do anything to protect their own interests in battle. He and Major Cardinal saw this as the best way to ensure combat readiness. The intent of all Second Division soldiers was to execute Cypher's commands for them to exercise civil disobedience against Dominion's constitution and laws, as well as any order from Adon Olam as commander-in-chief. They were trained to recognize Cypher as the true commander-in-chief, and it was every soldier's duty to rebel against Olam."

Following this opening statement, the chief magistrate continued by calling for testimonies from the rebels.

"I was at a meeting of the majors at which Cypher asked what I thought about Cur'sent and Cardinal being promoted to push the Second Division's agenda," testified the disgruntled Major Flips when he came to the stand. "I overheard Cypher promise them even higher ranks. The rest of us were like slaves, beaten and whipped for not performing the way they thought we should."

Corporal Amir took the stand next. "I was with Cypher and several majors at a division party when Cypher promised Cur'sent and Cardinal that he'd promote them to generals after the rebellion. I guess that's not going to happen now."

This produced a flurry of responses from the other gathered witnesses.

"Cardinal!" said Molly, one of Second Division's brigade commanders. "She's some commander. Just like Cur'sent. She demanded we insult, accuse, intimidate, and ridicule others to control them. She taught us to sweet talk, twist, and alter truth to get what we wanted... even lie. Why? Because that's the way of Cypher." She stared hard across the courtroom at Cardinal. "She drilled us for hours to respond with slander and intimidation. Cardinal said that Cypher was the truth."

Platoon commander Jamilia was next to testify. "Cardinal and Cur'sent ordered us to sidestep issues by calling others

Neanderthals, uneducated, ignorant, deplorable, filthy pigs, and stinking sewer rats. We were drilled in what they called the art of verbal belittlement." She frowned. "It's extremely toxic training, based on emotional and physical bullying, torment, and torture. Killings and executions. Under Cur'sent's intense intimidation, Cardinal demanded strict secrecy about this training."

More testimony came, this time from a young trooper. "We were told that we'd be wealthy and promoted to higher positions. We'd be supported by money gleaned from the taxes of businesses and confiscated property."

"The Second Division promoted the manipulation of truth at all levels," reported Bert, warrant officer third class. "They ran on half-truths, lies, and false information. This manipulation of truth was ordered by the upper command and promoted by In'Mutin to get the troops' buy-in."

Chief warrant officer Harvey spoke next "It was Cypher, with In'Mutin, who demanded the commanders, office staff, and troops give misleading information to headquarters. Cypher led by lying, stealing, and cheating to get what he wanted. No one trusted him."

When cross-examined, Cypher denied everything. "I didn't do it. I may have suggested fudging the numbers a bit, but it was the commanders and office staff who filed the false information. Not me. I'll not take responsibility for others. Lying was their choice. This wouldn't have happened if it weren't for Olam as commander-in-chief. It's his doing."

With that, Walking Eagle called the court to silence.

"We'll recess to clear the courtroom of anyone threatening the court," declared the chief magistrate.

For the second time in one week, the military police needed to be brought in to stop the witnesses from physically fighting.

Three weeks later, after consultations with Ellsworth with input from the review board, various lawyers, and advisors, Walking Eagle recommended that the court readjourn and delivered the sentence.

Once the court was quieted, the chief magistrate delivered the following judgment.

"All forces who rebelled, including officers, troops, office staff, and troops who defected to Cypher from Dominion forces, are herewith, now, and forever banished to Claydonia. I now declare this court adjourned."

Sentenced

The news was picked up immediately by the Dominion News Network. Anchor Andrew Weathersby excitedly broke into the regular newscast with the latest development.

"We have breaking news," said Weathersby. "Reporter Susy Slang is at the courthouse reporting on the sentencing of the rebels. Susy? What do you know at this time?"

"Yes, Andrew, we're here at the Supreme Court. It has been expected that there would be difficulties at the sentencing, but no one knew what would happen. We now know that two units of military police and four companies of infantry have been assigned to the courthouse and surrounding district. Absolute mayhem exploded after the sentence: total banishment to Claydonia. Fierce fighting is taking place right now to clear the courtroom of the angry mob."

Weatherby frowned. "We're having difficulty hearing you, Susy. Can you tell us more about what's happening?"

With that, the network lost its signal. Not until several days later was the broadcast restored, after emergency repairs to the communication lines.

"Susy, what's happening at the courthouse?" Weatherby asked.

"Yes, Andrew, I'm glad to say that we escaped with our lives. What I see is utter destruction. The courtroom is strewn with broken benches. The walls are damaged where chairs were hurled against them. The judge's bench and witness stand have been destroyed. Oh my goodness, it's terrible. Lights are hanging from the ceiling, doors ripped off their hinges, and windows smashed. I've learned that two platoons had to clear the final rioters with the help of court guards. Outside the courthouse, the military police faced off against inflamed rioters."

"Susy, that must look worse than a war zone."

"Yes. I've also been told that while this unfolded a series of other riots broke out at the detention centers. The chief magistrate's home has been vandalized, an attack stopped only by the intervention of Chief Olam's special operations unit. The Third Division was also called to help suppress the destruction."

"Susy, is there any indication of what will happen next?"

Susy took a moment to reply. "Yes, an unidentified source is indicating that when everything is under control, there are plans to begin the banishment of rebels. In the meantime, Dominion forces are being deployed to guard the detention facilities. Troops will also patrol the streets."

"Susy, can you tell us anything about where and when this banishment will be carried out?"

"Yes, I spoke to Chief Warrant Officer Hagans, who refused to answer that question. Back to you, Andrew."

Banishment

The banishment was being overseen by General Cha'el. At a meeting of majors, he addressed those under his command.

"We plan to exile the rebels from Dominion at 0800 hours tomorrow," Cha'el said. "Be at your posts with the required personnel. They're to leave with nothing. Have your personnel remove from them insignia, metals, and any other items related to Dominion. Dismissed."

At 0800 hours, the process began of moving the rebels out of the detention facilities. The first to depart were the top brass. Chief Olam handled these prisoners personally. As each was led to the inspection facilities, they were searched and addressed by the commander-in-chief.

The military police pushed Cypher to the front in defiance.

"Cypher, it is with a very heavy heart that we have come to this," said Olam. "I wish you well in your banishment. Consider your ways, and if possible make changes to become the person you have the potential to be."

Cypher spat on the ground. "Olam, I'll kill you for this."

Olam nodded, and with that the troops threw Cypher out of Dominion.

In a defiant display of power, Cypher fell like a streak of lightning to Claydonia. Afterward went Cur'sent, Cardinal, and In'Mutin, and their senior and junior officers, followed by their office staff and all remaining soldiers of the Second Division.

The location of Claydonia would make it extremely difficult for any of these rebels to find their way back to Dominion. And with their banishment, the land returned once again to an uneasy peace under Olam's direction.

New Agreement

After the banishment, Olam was deeply troubled by what had happened. As he walked along the river and looked to the southeast, he saw the dark clouds hanging ominously on the horizon.

I never again want Dominion to experience another uprising, he reasoned to himself. *To do this, I'll establish a new agreement to serve as the foundation of Dominion. This will help us all put the dark days behind us. I want all to know that they are safe and protected, to uphold everything Dominion stands for.*

He took the time to watch some pintail and ruddy ducks pass over the water. He wanted everyone in Dominion to be reassured that they would be free to do their best for others, including the expression of truth and execution of unbiased justice.

As he came to the split in the trail, he took the north branch and moved to the east, listening to the white-breasted nuthatch honking and enjoying life.

I must deal with the rebels and protect Dominion against their influence, he thought. *I also need to attract more personnel to Dominion, those who will contribute to its greatness.*

Coming to a particularly beautiful view, he sat on the riverbank and considered what would happen next. Even before the banishment, he had already established Claydonia as the future home of the Claydoms. The Claydoms, when they arrived, would be given the opportunity, if they chose, to be part of Dominion and its way of life. In fact, the essential element of his plan for Claydonia was for everyone to be free to choose, to have freedom of speech and be exactly who they wanted to be, wherever and whenever they wanted.

The same freedom would be extended to the rebels.

Once back at headquarters, Olam stepped into his office and jotted down some of his thoughts of the morning.

Once a Claydom chose to be spirit-oriented, they would be able to receive training to be brought to Dominion and eventually welcomed home.

New Beginning

As Cypher fell to Claydonia, he shook his clenched fists and swore filthy curses.

"Olam, you good for nothing filthy pig, you're a stinking sewer rat. If it's the last thing I do, I swear to annihilate you and what you stand for!"

He kicked rocks, beat his fists against trees, and ripped apart branches while unleashing curses more degrading than anything that had ever erupted from him.

When Cur'sent and Cardinal joined him on Claydonia, he flew at them in a wild rage. Cur'sent's anger also boiled over and they broke into a fight. Cardinal also joined the battle, fighting until all her energy was depleted.

Afterward, the combatants lay on the ground, exhausted and emotionally wounded. And that's where they were found as the rest of the rebels arrived, each and every one with bad temperaments and prone to vicious arguing and physical fighting.

"We've lost it all," the soldiers moaned. "We've lost our good times, and the money to do what we wanted when and where we wanted."

Time and again, Cur'sent and Cardinal confronted their former leader.

"Cypher, you promised a new order," demanded Cur'sent. "We backed you with everything we had. We swore allegiance with you, and look where that got us! You blatantly lied and said we had the forces, skills, and equipment to take Olam. Now here we are, outcasts in an alien place."

After another heated argument, with fists flying and cursing, Cypher stomped off, muttering to himself. "I'll eliminate those useless, no-good idiots."

"Hey, Cypher," said In'Mutin when the former agent tracked him down. "Ya had enough?"

Cypher flew at In'Mutin with a volley of profanity.

"Keep this up and all you'll do is offend the ones you need most right now," In'Mutin reminded him.

"You know as well as I that Cur'sent is out to be commander-in-chief," Cypher bellowed.

In'Mutin just walked away, "Have it your way, Cypher. You'll never get what you want. If you don't stop this stupidity, I'm gone."

That got Cypher's attention. "Okay, In'Mutin, have it your way! You always get your way."

"Right now, just go and do whatever you have to, but get the soldiers on your side. Without them, you'll never be their leader again."

Cypher left his agent and got together Cur'sent and Cardinal.

"I was crushed by what I've come through," he said to them. "You need to work together to settle my troops and find out where I am and what I need to do to get back to Dominion and eliminate Olam. In my new Dominion, I'm giving you both the top positions, with all the prestige, rewards, and pleasures that come with it."

"Cypher, but keep your anger under control," Cur'sent demanded.

Cardinal frowned "Yes! As long as you do that, we'll be okay."

"Okay," said Cypher. "Let's put together my New Dominion."

He ordered them to gather the highest-ranked officers, including three of the most influential—Zez, Abb, and Brutus.

Watching the majors leave, it occurred to him that the bond between Cur'sent and Cardinal had been cemented. They were now inseparable.

I'll coach them to assume even more important positions, Cypher thought. *They'll soon be focusing on their responsibility to establish my New Dominion.*

In only took an hour for Cur'sent and Cardinal to assemble the top commanders.

"Things didn't go as planned," Cypher told his commanders. "But I'm here now, so I'll get organized. I can still free Dominion from that useless, flea-bitten Olam. First I need to train my troops to stop fighting each other and instead focus on taking out Olam. While in detention, I've thought a lot about how to re-establish my forces. I'll begin with three divisions, with each one divided into brigades, battalions, companies, and platoons.

"General Zez, you will serve as commander of the First Division. You are a jealous defender of myself and my ways. For the Second Division, I assign General Abb. I need you in a top command post because you defended what I wanted during the rebellion. The Third Division commander will be General Brutus. You are a ruthless warrior. But I will need all three of you if I'm going to successfully take out Olam.

"All other officers will hold the same positions they've served in under the Second Division, so very little will change." Cypher turned to his adviser offhandedly. "In'Mutin, you'll be my special agent in charge of security. You'll be a private operative, collecting classified information on Olam and his dealings."

This wasn't quite the truth. In reality, he intended for In'Mutin to so serve as an internal spy, by snooping on his own personnel.

"I now command you all to assemble my troops. Generals, begin by finding shelter and gathering supplies. Dismissed!"

After watching the leaders disband, Cypher felt his wrath towards Olam grow even stronger. Before losing control of himself, he pulled In'Mutin aside.

"I've come to several realizations," he said to his friend. "It's taken a bit, but I now realize the immense roles Cur'sent and Cardinal have played in the fight so far. And now that I'm free of Olam and his demands, I believe I'll be more effective than ever."

Together, they began working on a written agreement that would shape his forces as they formed New Dominion.

It was only while working on this contract that an important realization came to Cypher. He threw up his hands in the air.

"Cur'sent!"

In'Mutin looked startled. "What do you mean?"

"I've been so focused on taking out Olam that I didn't realize until now what Cur'sent's name means." A warm thrill rushed through him. "Don't you see? 'The curse sent.' That describes him perfectly."

"And what about Cardinal? What does her name mean?"

He sent In'Mutin out to go find Cardinal and bring her to his office in his new military headquarters.

When the former major appeared, she was smiling seductively.

"Cardinal, remind me: what does your name mean?" Cypher asked.

She winked at him. "My name means, 'What persuades.' It doesn't matter what is said and done. It doesn't matter if something is the truth or a lie. No, the only thing that's important is what persuades. I'm the compelling cardinal lie that promotes all lies."

With this revelation out in the open, Cypher returned that smile. He could hardly restrain himself, now that he knew her potential.

She seductively left after saluting.

Cypher, now alone, thought through everything that had been handed to him since his division's banishment. He was finally the undisputed commander-in-chief of his own mighty force! What a day this was. He was so pleased that he could hardly contain his excitement.

He went into his new office feeling jubilant. Along the way, he passed In'Mutin and pulled him inside. In'Mutin rushed to catch up, taken by the urgency in his boss's manner.

"What's up, boss?"

"In'Mutin, I have a great future. By combining my ways with Cur'sent's and Cardinal's, I can get what I want. This combined personality will give me everything I need to win and eliminate my opposition. I've seen from you that I can use everyone and everything to gratify myself. I'll finetune my language and express myself more persuasively to build New Dominion. I've seen through your deception that absolute honesty and truth are only used to lure others."

In'Mutin smiled. "Cypher, you've learned well the power of manipulating the truth."

"My trained forces are a powerful element. They must do what I demand. And if they don't, I'll eliminate them to encourage the other troops' obedience."

"You're commander-in-chief already, but why not appoint yourself as ruler of New Dominion?"

"Good, In'Mutin. First I'll declare my new order. Then I'll appoint myself Supreme and Wise Ruler." He paused to think. "I'm also ordering an all-troop parade in two weeks."

Symbol of Power

When the day of the parade arrived, Cypher stood tall as he stepped up to the podium. He grasped the podium firmly and scanned the troops.

"I congratulate you for your work in developing New Dominion and for your hard training," he announced in a booming voice. "I know you're the mightiest force ever known. Our new territory will be known as New Order Dominion, and I will call it NO Dom. It's what I fought Olam for."

A loud, resounding cheer raced over the land. Only when the soldiers settled did Cypher continue.

"I am Supreme and Wise Ruler of NO Dom. Indeed, I am the supreme power of the universe. There's no power or force greater than me. I am the power that created NO Dom. I am the greatest creator of all. I have been, I am, and I will always be. I am eloquent in appearance and position. I am intelligent. I have integrity. I am honesty. I am truth. No one is grander. What I stand for, what I do, is for the best—for *your* best!"

After this, he dismissed his troops.

However, in the coming days he realized that the troops didn't seem to respect him as their newly appointed Supreme and Wise Ruler.

"In'Mutin, if I didn't need these imbecile troops, I'd exterminate them all," he said to his friend as they lounged in his office.

"Why?"

"Look at them! They won't train and they think they're entitled to everything. All I hear is their talk of Dominion and how great that stinking Olam is!" He furrowed his brow, feeling troubled. "Come with me to inspect my troops, In'Mutin. Let's watch their training. I'll see my training facilities for myself."

They left the building and made their way to the nearby training grounds, where soldiers were hard at work. He gazed in pride at the display.

"Hey, Cypher, you did all this," In'Mutin marvelled.

"Yeah. I've created it all. I've supplied everything that's needed to sustain life here, setting up NO Dom in all its splendour and glory. And yet!"

Cypher threw his hands up in disgust. He angrily kicked a rock, causing it to crash into a low bush and startle the snake that slithered out from beneath it.

In'Mutin brightened, as though he'd had an idea. "Have you thought about using a symbol?"

"Yeah," Cypher said, understanding where his friend was going with this. "Vipers are feared. The snake is its own creature, cunning and strong. In'Mutin! This snake's going to be the symbol of my authority! I'll make a crown representing the snake."

Rushing back to headquarters, Cypher gathered his artisans and demanded them to make his crown.

Some time passed, and when his crown was finally presented to him he was alarmed by its impact of authority and splendour. The sleek serpent had its tail drooped at the back, its body encircling the crown. In front, the creature's head was raised upright and flared, symbolizing aggressive authority and might. The masterpiece sparkled with jewels and was delicately lined with the softest furs of wild ermine. What a sight it was!

The head artisan respectfully handed it to him. Cypher then rose in reverence and, with trembling hands, studied his crown. He carefully and lovingly caressed it, feeling every part.

"What a beautiful creation I've made…"

He hesitated as this spectacle glowed before him. He then placed his masterpiece onto his own head. As the weight of his beautiful sparking crown came upon him, his mind exploded with pride and authority.

"Now I truly am Supreme and Wise Ruler of NO Dom! There's none like me, nor will there ever be another to wear my crown with my authority, my power, and my glory!"

The artisan presented him with a mirror, which Cypher seized. He took a deep breath and slowly raised the mirror to glimpse himself again in all his splendour.

"What a chief I am," he quietly uttered. "Handsome, brilliant, powerful, and now splendid in all my ways."

In'Mutin nodded approvingly. "There's no other!"

Authority Conferred

Later that week, Cypher called Cur'sent and Cardinal into his office. He wore his new crown for them to behold for the first time.

"Here's how I'll present my authority to the forces, so they'll respect me," he said.

Cypher immediately noticed their confusion at his crown, so he sought to calm their concerns.

"I'm having headdresses made for each of you as well," Cypher said. "They'll confer respect."

Cardinal smiled, but it was forced. "If you think it'll work."

"I guess it's all right," said Cur'sent in disgust.

Both of Cypher's top generals left the office worried about their boss's selfish ambition.

"Perhaps that crown is only for show," Cardinal remarked, trying to persuade herself.

"He really wouldn't assume such a powerful authority," Cur'sent muttered. "Would he? I mean, we know he's nothing without our authority over the troops. He'll get over this."

But while Cur'sent and Cardinal spoke amongst themselves, Cypher was already rushing back to his artisans. Once the new headdresses were ready, he called for a new parade.

At the parade, he stood at the podium and called for his chief warrant officer to bring forward the crown and the other two headdresses.

Once Cur'sent and Cardinal had joined him on the stage, Cypher addressed his soldiers.

He started by installing Cur'sent and Cardinal as Chief of Defence Staff and Chief of Defence Staff Advisor respectively. He then turned to the commanders and prepared to give them their new assignments.

"I will now honour General Cur'sent for his brilliant leadership. With this new headdress, you will know that he is my Chief of Defence Staff."

There were a few claps, but no great ovation.

"I now honour General Cardinal for her diligent training in communications. With this headdress, you will be known as my Chief of Defence Staff Advisor."

He paused for more cheers and then nodded to the chief warrant officer, who then handed the snake crown to Cur'sent and Cardinal. Together, the generals placed the crown on Cypher's head.

After the crowning, a cold, awkward silence swept over the troops. Some looked upon him in disdain. Many others stood in uncomfortable awe.

"Good grief," the soldiers muttered with seething anger. "What's next? This is absurd."

There was much complaining about these new symbols of power, but Cypher ignored their hateful reactions.

"I represent NO Dom as commander-in-chief. I know what's best for you! You can trust me. I will make sure all will be clothed, all will be fed, all will be housed, and all will receive top medical care. I alone will do this for you!"

He commanded his generals to dismiss their divisions.

"What a sensation!" Cypher crowed in his office after the parade. "What a thrill being crowned Supreme and Wise Ruler… yet I feel my forces didn't like my new image. Nor do they accept me for what I'm doing for them."

Pushback

Over the coming days, the grumbling and discontent of Cypher's forces made the training lacklustre. At every level, troops muttered and complained bitterly. The number of soldiers in sickbay rose. Even Cypher's generals refused to call their divisions to regular duties.

In fact, Cur'sent and Cardinal avoided Cypher. They sarcastically and bluntly answered him when asked for input, then returned to their alleged work.

Cypher sulked as he pondered why his forces didn't accept him. He watched his troops' morale plummet.

"Those stupid, idiotic, brainless troops have no right to disagree with me," he grumbled.

"You never gave us any warning," Cardinal said in a sarcastic tone. "You just did it!"

Cypher snapped back. "I'm Supreme and Wise Ruler of NO Dom!"

"So what? If you want us to buy in, you have ta let us know what's up! Don't just throw stuff at us. Why'd you choose that slimy snake? Why the headdress? Why the big show at the parade?"

With that, she stomped out, slamming the door behind her.

Cypher felt highly wounded. "What do I need her for? I'll eliminate her right now!" But his anger cooled over time. "I can't. But if she wasn't critical to what I want, I'd kill her right now."

He sat behind his desk moping, fuming, and cursing everything around him.

In'Mutin stepped in while he wallowed. "You know you're Supreme and Wise Ruler."

"Yer right! I am. I'll demand my rightful honour."

In the middle of his dilemma, he decided to approach the situation differently. "I'll just con them into thinking I'm doing the best for them! When I was commander of the Second Division, I was highly respected. I'll demand that respect now."

"Cypher, you're the most splendid commander-in-chief there is."

"And I'll show them that I'm their Supreme and Wise Ruler. I'll have them believing I'm doing their best by taking the focus off myself."

"What do you mean?"

"I'll introduce the snake as supreme leader. I'll give the snake my attributes. Then I can be who I am… and the snake can take the blame. That snake will develop the contract with my forces. 'What can I do?' I'll say. 'I'm only the snake's representative. I do what the snake directs me to do!' But I'll have to give the snake a name. How about Snake, Dragon of Old, the Powerful Darkness?"

Cypher grabbed his written speech from his desk drawer and began to rewrite it.

"Snake, Dragon of Old, the Powerful Darkness is eternal. Snake has been, is, and will always be. Snake is the eternal creator of all. Snake created NO Dom, set all plans in motion, and gives all direction. Snake gives laws and ordinances. Snake supplies everything needed for life, like food, clothing, and shelter. Snake provides for the people's well-being and health. Snake supplies all employment. Snake is in full control of everyone's lives. Snake is intelligent and all-wise, full of integrity, truth, and honesty. Snake is love and compassion. Snake is eloquent in appearance. He sees all and knows all. Yes, Snake, Dragon of Old, the Powerful Darkness, has a driving desire to see the best for everyone. No one is greater or wiser."

In'Mutin slapped his friend on the back. "Congratulations. The wording of this declaration to your forces couldn't be better."

Next, Cypher called Cur'sent and Cardinal into his office.

"Cardinal, I've been thinking about what you said. I apologize for not letting you two know what I was doing. From now on, I'll keep you updated." Cypher indicated the crown on his head. "You see, this crown represents Snake. I'll be subject to Snake."

The two officers felt guilty for being so blunt with Cypher, so they quickly agreed.

"Thank you," Cardinal said. "I appreciate your honesty and straightforwardness with us."

Cur'sent nodded. "Sure. We'll make this work."

Together, they left his office. But between them they conspired to exercise control over everything Cypher did, since they were the intermediaries between him and the troops.

Cypher next called together his generals, and also informed them about his new plan to be subject to Snake, doing only as Snake directed him.

He then asked them for suggestions.

"Sir, a full parade should be called to inform the troops of this change," said General Abb.

"Thank you," Cypher said. "Do you need anything from me to build your divisions?"

They were taken back, as this was the first time Cypher had asked them for this kind of input.

General Brutus was cautious. "Sir, could we get back to you on this?"

"Yes. Dismissed!"

Feeling ecstatic with how his plan was working out, Cypher instructed Cur'sent and Cardinal to organize yet another parade.

SNAKE

Cur'sent and Cardinal scheduled the parade to take place within the month, on a Wednesday. The troops would be ready for review at 0800 hours, and the commander-in-chiefs would follow at 1100 hours. The soldiers would be dismissed at 1200 hours.

Cypher beamed when they informed him of the plans. "You two have done a fabulous job. I appreciate your proficient handling of this task. Cur'sent, would you do the honours of welcoming the troops? And Cardinal, would you invite the generals to report? Then I'll address the troops. Thank you. A job well done. Dismissed."

There was a subdued formality on the day of the parade as the forces marched in, formed up, and were reviewed by each general.

Chief of Defence Staff Cur'sent was the first to speak from the podium. "Welcome, troops. It's a great day with an excellent review. Well done! I now ask my Chief of Defence Staff Advisor, Cardinal, to join me."

There was a hardy cheer as Cardinal came to the stage.

"It's an honour to welcome our generals to report on their divisions," Cardinal cut in.

Each of the generals—Zez, Abb, and Brutus—were called up to speak in turn. Once the commanders were finished, Cur'sent returned to the podium to introduce their boss.

"Now please welcome our commander-in-chief, our Supreme and Wise Ruler, Cypher, to deliver a state of New Order Dominion address."

Cypher appeared wearing his crown. He stepped forward with his chest out and head held high. He gripped the podium and looked with satisfaction over the forces before him.

"Thank you for doing a fantastic and dedicated job of organizing the parade," he said, nodding to Cur'sent and Cardinal. "Thank you also to each general for your leadership. And I also thank each member of our forces for your diligence. Every soldier is deeply appreciated for working to make New Order Dominion the greatest place it can be."

He took a moment to pause and gather himself.

"I must, in all humility, apologize for my lack of protocol at the last parade. I didn't conduct myself as I should have. Through consultation with my chiefs and generals, I have come here today to clarify the standing of New Order Dominion."

The troops seemed to believe him.

"To all my forces, you are the greatest!" he continued, raising his voice. "You are the mightiest force there is. How proud I am today!"

A robust cheer rose from the troops.

"I have great news for you. Not only are you the mightiest force, but you now have a mighty leader who will prepare you for even greater things. This new leader will take you into battle!" He paused again. "Your new leader is Snake, Dragon of Old, the Powerful Darkness."

Yet again a mighty cheer rose. Cypher only continued his conning once the applause had faded.

"Let it be known today and forever that our mighty leader, Snake, Dragon of Old, the Powerful Darkness, is eternal. Snake has been, is, and will always be. Snake is the eternal creator of all. Snake created NO Dom, set all plans in motion, and gives all direction. Snake gives laws and ordinances. Snake supplies everything needed for life, like food, clothing, and shelter. Snake provides for your well-being and health. Snake supplies all employment. Snake is in full control of everyone's lives. Snake is intelligent and all-wise, full of integrity, truth, and honesty. Snake is love and compassion. Snake is eloquent in appearance. He sees all and knows all. Yes, Snake, Dragon of Old, the Powerful Darkness, has a driving desire to see the best for everyone. No one is greater or wiser."

The cheers from the crowd flowed across the universe like an enormous, unstoppable wave, dark and ominous.

"Snake, Dragon of Old, the Powerful Darkness, has installed me as Supreme and Wise Ruler of NO Dom. He has given me this crown so I can represent him! He is all-powerful, to be worshipped and obeyed." Cypher removed his crown, set it before him, and bowed down. "I'm eternally obedient to you, Snake, Dragon of Old, the Powerful Darkness!"

In unison, the forces shouted: "Snake, Dragon of Old, the Powerful Darkness!"

Once Cypher had saluted the crown, Cur'sent quickly dismissed the excited and jubilant forces. Now they had a true ruler: Snake, Dragon of Old, the Powerful Darkness. The shadowy darkness from the east had seeped even deeper into life here in Claydonia.

Feeling jubilant at the parade's success, Cypher immediately met with In'Mutin in his office back at headquarters.

"In'Mutin, I've never known such a pleasure. I've won… and won bigtime. They've bought into my declaration that NO

Dom is the supreme power in the universe, with nothing superior. They believe that everything this nation stands for is for their own good."

"Cypher, I congratulate your success. You're the pinnacle of commanders-in-chief."

"Even in my new power, I still hate that conman Olam. I'll soon demand more ruthless battle techniques, allowing me to take Dominion. When the troops are properly trained, I'll finally destroy that filthy pig."

Freedom of Choice

Back in Dominion, Chief Olam and his forces repaired the damage from the costly civil war. The country had returned to a cautious peace.

Olam called together all of his generals to assess the current situation.

"It's disturbing me to watch Cypher's egotistic manipulation of his forces," Olam remarked.

Cha'el nodded. "I've noticed that, too. By focusing on himself, he isn't seeing the settling darkness falling on him and his forces."

"Members of our joint taskforce have been keeping a close watch on Cypher and his activities," said Rafal. "Some of his soldiers are disgruntled troops, objecting to his new god and his selfish ways. He is betraying many of his own obligations to his troops. I think they know their time of punishment is coming and secretly plan to overthrow Cypher. Or, when they have support, they may even try to escape Claydonia and set up a new nation."

Olam then set out to explain his larger plan for what would happen next.

"Unknown to Cypher even before his uprising, I've worked out a plan for the future development of our forces. In doing this, I established Claydonia. Many Claydoms will eventually live here, and they will one day prove their allegiance to me and join Dominion. But the rebels are also part of my plan. That's why I exiled them to Claydonia. During their exile, they will be in our sights while feeling free of our control. They will be able to influence those Claydoms who come to live in the land…"

A few weeks later, as Olam and his generals walked east along the river, they pondered the future of Dominion.

"Dominion is a vast and spectacularly beautiful expanse with a small population," the chief said in a quiet voice. "My greatest desire is for many more Claydoms to enjoy Dominion and its grandeur."

"Do you know how many will come?" Stren asked.

"Not as yet. But I've prepared a strategic plan for Dominion to fulfill their dream of finding a place of true contentment, peace, and freedom. You see, if one desires to have freedom of choice, there must be no limitations placed on their choice. Anything less than this wouldn't be true freedom. This is my statement of purpose."

General Barac nodded. "As commander of the Second Division, Cypher knew about this. He was trained to understand all about freedom of choice."

"Yes, Barac," said Olam. "This is also why, with great sadness, I allowed him and his troops to rebel. I wouldn't do anything to destroy anyone's freedom of choice, even if they choose to attack Dominion."

Cha'el frowned at hearing this. "When Cypher deliberately attacked us, we stood to defend ourselves with all our power and might. If freedom of choice was lost, all of Dominion would fall to darkness."

Eastern Darkness

Life in NO Dom settled into a mundane existence. With his bloated ego, Cypher was unaware of the self-serving actions of Cur'sent and Cardinal, who over time gained immense authority and power over their troops. Cypher was distracted by his work to finetune Snake, Dragon of Old, the Powerful Darkness, to be worshipped.

In the meantime, Cur'sent was enjoying the perks of his elite position. One day he called Cardinal to his office for a conference.

"We seem to have lots of time," Cur'sent began. "The troops won't be ready for battle for a long while. And if they don't obey our commands, we can eliminate them."

Cardinal smiled. "Yes. Besides, the troops are getting better at adapting to Cypher's ways of lying, stealing, and cheating."

"I immensely enjoy this game of outwitting others to get what we want. I get such a thrill out of it… you know, the mayhem. The troops are constantly squabbling and even breaking into fights over their perceived rights. Our commanders are relentless in their drive to make the troops more intimidating. Their punishments are ruthless."

Indeed, as they looked out the window they saw that the darkness was very thick. And yet everyone here in Claydonia now seemed to accept that this was normal.

Invasion

As Olam's plans continued to unfold, he decided, after consulting with his top brass, to deploy a unit to conduct reconnaissance in Claydonia and determine whether Cypher was using the proposed landing area. These troops' mission would be to secure information about the land's condition and determine how Cypher's forces were getting along.

The special operations team landed on Claydonia in the midst of a heavy, eerie darkness.

A platoon of Cypher's troops were nearby just in time to catch sight of Dominion's soldiers come ashore along a quiet gulf along the northwestern coast of Claydonia.

"Major Phillips, I just spotted a team of enemy troops land at the gulf!" came a radioed report from one of the privates who'd seen the landing firsthand.

"Did they see you?" the major demanded.

"Don't know."

"Okay, private." At his outpost, the major placed a call to one of his top sergeants. "Order all troops in that zone muster at the southern bend in the river."

The sergeant reported back instantly. "Yes, sir."

Phillips' next call was to signals. "Dispatch a communication to headquarters right away: 'Unknown troops seen invading.'"

"Yes, sir. Dispatch sent!"

Two days later, a military dispatch crashed through the front doors of NO Dom's headquarters.

"Get Cur'sent," shouted the dispath. "I gotta see him *now*."

The officers stationed at the front doors responded by staring openly, their mouths open in surprise.

"Don't sit there. Get Cur'sent!"

"But you can't see him right now," said the office administrator. "He's in a meeting and can't be disturbed."

A heated volley of cursing and swearing echoed through the hallways as the troops began to bicker amongst themselves. The sound reached all the way to Cur'sent's conference room, disturbing him.

The Chief of Defence Staff threw open the conference room door and demanded that the yelling stop. "What's all the fuss about?"

"Sir, I must tell you—!'

"Shut up!" Cur'sent exploded. "Wait 'til I'm finished."

With that, the Chief of Defence Staff viciously slammed the door shut and continued with his business.

Four hours later, Cur'sent, Cardinal, and the generals emerged from their meeting looking and sounding disgruntled. They walked towards the front of the building, passing the waiting dispatch.

The dispatch stood and saluted. "Sir, I must—"

"When I'm finished," barked Cur'sent.

The top brass walked out the front doors, going about their busy morning. It wasn't until two hours later that Cur'sent and Cardinal returned.

"There's been an invasion, sir," shouted the dispatch.

Cur'sent stopped in his tracks and demanded answers. "Why didn't you tell me? Who's invading? Where?"

"At the gulf!"

"How many invaders are there?"

"We don't know."

Cur'sent became increasingly agitated. "Who is it?"

"Don't know."

"Why don't you know?"

"Wasn't told, sir. All I was to report is that troops were seen invading."

In the ensuing chaos, Cur'sent and Cardinal rushed up to Cypher's office, where the boss was found behind his desk.

"There's a door, you know," Cypher spit when they barged in on him. "Knock next time!"

"We've been invaded!" shouted Cur'sent.

Cypher let out a string of curses. "That stinking sewer rat, Olam... that filthy pig..." He jumped to his feet. "All generals to the war room!"

War Room

When the generals arrived at the war room, they discovered that the room was missing the required protocol. General Zez flew into an instant rage.

"Why don't you idiots have this place in order?" Zez demanded of the other two generals. "Do I have to do everything?"

"Then why wasn't it done?" growled Brutus.

Frusrated, Zez turned and punched Brutus in the face. Abb subsequently came to Zez's defence, who took offence and fought back. It didn't take long for complete mayhem to break out. They hurled fierce curses at each other.

In this seething chaos, Cypher entered, with the crown upon his head. Upon seeing their boss, everyone turned on him like a pack of wolves.

"Cypher, you're an idiot!" bellowed Zez.

Abb lit into him. "You're dumber than a stinking dead skunk! Why wasn't the war room ready?"

Brutus shoved Abb and Zez aside. "Cypher, your only concern is for your own lowdown, filthy, flea-bitten hide."

Cypher whipped off his crown. "I assigned war room preparedness to Cur'sent and Cardinal," he bellowed. "They probably passed it off to their office staff, and I wouldn't be surprised if it somehow got passed all the way to you incompetents. In everyone's blundering about, no one actually did the work. So shut up and take responsibility for your own failure!"

When Cur'sent and Cardinal arrived with the required files, they still couldn't get to work. Fists and boots flew as they battled over placing blame.

"I command everyone to control their anger," Cur'sent yelled several hours into the contest. "If you don't, I'll demote you all to latrine duty for a month."

With this came a general scrambling to get the place in order and gather intelligence about the invasion.

The next day, the leaders of NO Dom met to plan their action against the invasion.

"To get some direction, let's assume that unknown troops came to get a lay of the land," began Abb.

But still they fought over procedures. This heated debate continued into the night amidst allegations of ineptitude, downright stupidity, and deliberate negligence of duty.

It was Cur'sent who finally broke the logjam. "I'm ordering an immediate alert of all our forces to counteract this invading force."

In a great turmoil, the troops attempted to mobilize in the parade square. Supplies and equipment were strewn about as the commanding officers tried to organize the units to a state of readiness. It took several hours before the soldiers were ready to be deployed.

"We've lost so much time. Why even bother going?" Zez demanded. "Our deployment can't be successful."

Cur'sent ignored her. "All units, form up."

"General Abb, deploy your division to the sight of the invasion," Cardinal barked angrily.

"With all due respect, ma'am, where is that exactly?" Zez demanded.

Yet more confusion erupted as Zez came at her superiors, cursing and yelling as she threw punches.

Cur'sent finally got the enraged general under control. "General Zez, stand down or you'll be demoted to dungeon duty." He turned to one of the more composed Abb. "General, deploy your division to the west. And don't return until NO Dom is secured."

Once Abb's units had cleared the parade square, Cardinal issued further orders. "General Brutus, deploy the Third Division to the gulf. And Zez! Deploy your division to defend headquarters and oversee the supply chains to our troops in the field."

Third Division

General Brutus was known by his troops for his vicious command style. They called him the Brute.

After two hours of marching northwest, the Brute finally called them to a halt. "Stand down, troops! Scouts, check forward advancement."

A few minutes later, the scouts returned. "All clear, sir."

"Form up," the Brute ordered. "Forward march!"

Amongst NO Dom's Third Division, with Brutus in charge, were two specially trained members: Tum and Bed, two huge and rugged sergeants. They were cousins and came from a lineage of mean, illiterate troops despised by all. Wherever they and their associates went, they smugly left a trail of terror and destruction. In fact, over the past months their psychopathic exploits had produced a vast swath of devastation through Claydonia.

Tum loved to mock and torment his enemies, especially as they cowered in front of him. Bed lived to inflict pure, unadulterated agony, both for his own sinister delight and because there was nothing more satisfying than rendering a hapless victim lifeless.

"Set camp!" barked the Brute.

After camp was set, the Brute sent out another unit of scouts. These scouts didn't take long to respond with news that the troops had come to within striking distance of the invasion point along the northwestern gulf.

In the morning, just before dawn, the Brute mobilized the troops and prepared them for action.

"Troops, be diligent in what you see and hear," he ordered. "Silent advance!"

The troops advanced for about an hour before the Brute once again called for a halt to their march.

"Spread out, but stay close. Absolute silence! Wait for attack orders!"

The soldiers now waited and listened for any sound of the enemy in the cold darkness.

Engagement

When Dominion's special operations team first landed in Claydonia, they encountered a heavy darkness. Silence drifted over the entire land.

The mission was of such importance. Because Cypher hated Olam and desired to take Dominion by force, and from the information received about the landing area, Olam and his generals decided that an immediate arrival on Claydonia would be best.

"Rafal, you'll command the First and Sixth Divisions," Olam ordered. "They will remain for the protection of Headquarters. Fifth Division, Barac, you're on standby when needed. Advancing from Dominion is the First Division's Joint Taskforce, backed by Cha'el's Third Division and Stren's Fourth Division."

When formed up, he shouted, "Move out for Claydonia!"

Once they had landed, the commander-in-chief addressed them again.

"Hold and listen for any movements indicating that Cypher's forces may be in the area," Olam said.

As the troops waited, they began hearing movement to the front and left of their position. In response, Olam signaled for the First Division's joint taskforce to advance. They moved forward.

Upon hearing and seeing the approach of Dominion soldiers, the Brute issued new orders.

"Tum, Bed... attack!"

Immediately, an eruption of furious battle raged. The sounds of fierce fighting shattered the morning's unnerving silence.

"Third and Fourth Divisions, advance!" Olam ordered.

As he and his troops burst through the darkness, they encountered Sergeant Tum, snarling violently and leaping at him. With mighty strength, however, Olam flung Tum aside and defended himself from Bed's grotesque appearance. The struggle against these two enemies was immense, but Olam managed with the aid of the powerful Joint Taskforce Major Sep to turn the tide despite the prevailing darkness.

Soon Tum and Bed had both been bound.

Cha'el, at the head of Dominion's Third Division, advanced straight to the front, where he succeeded in capturing the Brute. Many prisoners of war were taken into custody and taken to a makeshift detention zone near the gulf where the Dominion forces had first landed.

With the Fourth Division, Stren swung left and captured several companies more. In fact, most of Cypher's forces soon found themselves encircled.

It soon became clear that the battle was won. In the aftermath, Olam ordered his troops to pursue NO Dom's fleeing soldiers.

"Search the immediate area and bring any prisoners of war to the detention area," ordered Cha'el.

With the landing area secured and NO Dom's Third Division in full retreat, Olam advised Cha'el to advance into the surrounding countryside. This new advance soon engaged another enemy division, this one led by General Abb, who had been rushing to the Brute's defence.

Once disbanded, the survivors on Cypher's side beat a hasty retreat back to headquarters.

Olam placed Cha'el in charge of looking after the captives while Stren's division pursued NO Dom survivors. Once Stren had returned from his mission, he was put in charge of the prisoners of war.

"Generals, set camp, stand down, and post guards for our protection for the night," Olam commanded. "Dismissed."

The following morning, by 0800 hours, Olam, Cha'el, and the entire Third Division were advancing towards Cyphers headquarters.

Cypher, Cur'sent, and Cardinal met in the boss's office, devastated as they watched their wounded and depleted forces stagger in and overload the sickbay.

"General Zez, place the First Division on high alert," Cypher ordered. "They will need to defend headquarters!"

As NO Dom brass worked to sort out the lies and misinformation from truth, Dominion's Third Division came into sight of their target. They stopped outside of headquarters and the parade square.

From inside the building, Cur'sent pointed out the invaders. "Cypher, look! Olam and Cha'el have come in person. We're both outmaneuvered and outnumbered."

Intense arguments broke out between the cornered leaders of NO Dom.

"Zez, go out and stall them as long as possible," Cur'sent ordered. "Perhaps we can give ourselves time to mount a defence."

Zez saluted. "Yes, sir!"

Olam smiled when he saw the general appear at the front doors of NO Dom's headquarters and marched towards them.

"Zez, it's good to see you," the chief called.

In the ensuing awkward moment, Zez realized that Olam knew why she was standing there. She looked up and clumsily asked, "What are your terms of surrender?"

"What are the terms Cypher, Cur'sent, and Cardinal have agreed on?"

"We have none yet."

"Here's a proposal," said Olam. "Right now, command your troops to lay down arms and battle equipment and form up on the parade square. Dominion's forces will surround them and take them into custody as prisoners of war."

Knowing that Zez was underhanded, Cha'el raised his hand to demonstrate that Dominion's forces were ready to attack.

Zez was stunned to realize she could be about to witness the immediate destruction of NO Dom. She didn't quite know how to react.

"General Cha'el, are you ready to order an attack?" Olam asked.

"Yes, sir! At your command!"

"Cha'el, advance troops."

Cha'el turned and shouted, "Troops, advance fifty paces!"

The immense sound and sight of thousands of heavily armed troops advancing rattled Zez. She stood before this immense military force and heard the orders of her division's commanders to defend NO Dom.

Just as the confrontation was about to break out, the front doors opened and Cypher rushed out, flanked by Cur'sent, Cardinal, and Abb.

Olam and Cha'el advanced anyway, forcing Zez to step back. They then came face to face with Cypher, where they halted. Dominion's forces had surrounded the enemy.

Cha'el called a halt. The tension was so high now that the general could hear the desperation in Cypher's breathing.

"Olam, what are you doing?" Cypher demanded.

"Dominion, prepare weapons!" Olam ordered, then turned to his enemy. "Cypher, what's with the crown?"

This question shook Cypher and he didn't respond.

"Here's what I'm going to do," Olam said. "I can punish you by eliminating you right now for your rebellion in Dominion. Or you can surrender your troops. Which will it be?"

Cardinal opened her mouth to speak, but Olam stopped her.

"This is not your time to persuade." Olam once again turned to Cypher. "Cypher, you want someone else to make the decisions, don't you? So you can blame them? Well, it's up to you to decide the future now—for you and your troops. What will it be?"

Cur'sent grew frustrated with Cypher's hesitation. "Make up your stinking mind, Cypher! Make a choice! We're surrounded! Don't you understand? We're done, finished, because of your stupid, selfish incompetency. Your greed. Your self-centeredness. You got us here, Cypher... now do something."

Cur'sent reared back his arm and slugged Cypher in the shoulder.

Cypher stumbled back from the blow and grabbed Cur'sent by his tunic. "You want me to do something? Okay, I'll do something." He turned to Olam. "They're all yours."

As Cypher turned to leave, Cardinal kicked his legs out from under him. The crown fell off Cypher's head and tumbled to the ground. Cardinal was so mad that she kicked it clear across the parade square, watching it tumble.

Olam smiled. "I don't want them, Cypher. They're yours. You deal with them."

Zez picked up Cypher's crown, dusted it off, and placed it back onto Cypher's head. She then stepped back and saluted him.

Olam allowed this event to sink in. "Cypher, give orders for your troops to lay down their arms and equipment."

Cypher stood tall and squared his shoulder. "Cur'sent, disarm my troops."

"Yes, sir." Cur'sent turned to the generals. "General Zez, General Abb. Disarm the troops and place the weapons in storage."

They both saluted. "Yes, sir!"

Cha'el looked on, suspicious. "Troops, watch their disarmament closely and be ready for any acts of aggression."

But very soon Cypher's forces had all been disarmed.

"Cha'el, move our troops to a safe distance and assign guards to watch after NO Dom's headquarters," said Olam. "We'll also need to keep an eye on the parade square, munitions, armament facilities, and military quarters. Then we'll set up camp nearby."

Once disarmed, Olam and Cha'el met with Cypher, Cur'sent, Cardinal, Zez, and Abb in the parade square.

"The time for your surrender is set for 0900 hours four days from today," said Olam. He turned to Cypher, Cur'sent, and Cardinal. "During that time, you'll be placed under house arrest in separate locations. You'll not contact or communicate with each other or your troops. If you do, you'll be jailed at once. Do you understand me?"

All three of them nodded.

Olam turned his attention to the generals. "General Zez, General Abb. Inform your troops of the schedule and ensure no one attempts to escape custody. Do you understand?"

Again, the generals nodded. But Olam wasn't done yet.

"General Zez, you will report any difficulties or needs that may arise to General Cha'el. General Abb, you will erect a meeting tent with tables and chairs for the upcoming surrender talks. Dismissed!"

These senior officers were all taken away.

Return March

Once Cha'el had made all the arrangements for the leaders' detention, he found Olam once again at their encampment.

"Cha'el, how soon can the rest of our troops be moved here, along with all other prisoners of war?"

"If we sent support troops at once, hopefully within three days. One day there. One day to prepare and move out. Then one day to march here by evening."

"Thank you. Let's do it."

"Yes, sir!"

Within the hour, a platoon of support troops was back on its way west to the landing area on the western shores of Claydonia. They arrived the following day, surprising Stren and the rest of his troops.

"General Stren, General Cha'el reports a cease in action," reported the platoon major. "All troops and prisoners of war are to be moved to NO Dom headquarters. It will be a hard day's march to make headquarters by evening on the second day."

"Thank you, Major."

Due to his belligerent demands for immediate release, General Brutus stirred up the emotions of Tum and Bed. After some time, however, these soldiers were all secured and placed under heavy guard.

"Move out," Stren ordered the next day after 1200 hours. The first hours of marching were awkward, with the Dominion troops working hard to keep their NO Dom prisoners of war on their feet.

However, Brutus, Tum, and Bed refused to cooperate. At every turn, they introduced confusion into the operation.

As the first day of marching darkened, Stren called a halt and set camp. At this, the prisoners posed a great challenge to Dominion forces by launching attacks against them. After an hour of vicious battle, the Dominion troops managed to secure the combatants.

Once secured, Brutus, Tum, and Bed began screaming like a herd of wild banshees. To get relief from this horrid noise, each had to be gagged and hooded.

The next morning, while preparations were being made to depart again, the three agitators were tied up. If they refused to walk, they would be dragged.

It was extremely late when the lights of NO Dom headquarters came into sight.

On seeing his troops' arrival, Olam felt satisfied. "Cha'el, take charge of the prisoners of war and bring them to the same holding area as Zez and Abb."

Once this was done, Zez and Abb took charge of the prisoners.

Zez put her hands on her hips. "Whoever can walk, go to your barracks."

"Medics take the wounded immediately to sickbay," Abb ordered.

Zez turned to Brutus, Tum, Bed, surprised to see their clothes torn and ragged. "Why are they in such bad shape? And why are they secured by rope?"

After hearing of their constant defiance, she lit into them with such volatile profanity and threats that they soon wanted to desert. There was much tongue-lashing and threats of dismemberment. Zez eventually had one of her own guards throw all three into the deepest, darkest dungeon available.

Before retiring for the night, Olam pulled Cha'el and Stren aside and explained that he wanted to gather all of Dominion's forces to headquarters for security purpose. It was of paramount important that their numbers be large enough to squelch any uprising that could arise during the coming negotiations around Cypher's surrender.

Olam also called Zez for a quick meeting.

"Zez, I need you to ensure General Brutus is presentable so that he can appear at the coming surrender talks."

"Why Brutus?" Zez demanded. "He's caused so many problems and deserves to rot in prison! Or better yet, executed!"

"No. He must be at the meetings tomorrow. Specifically, at 0900 hours."

SURRENDER

In the morning, at 0800 hours, Olam asked for Cypher, Cur'sent, and Cardinal to be escorted to the meeting tent that Abb had readied for their use. At 0855 hours, Olam marched in with Cha'el, Stren, and Hagans. Everyone stood.

"Be seated, Olam said, slowly looking from one face to the next. "It's with some sadness that we're here today. May I remind you all that you're a defeated force? Cypher, Supreme and Wise Ruler—or Snake, Dragon of Old, the Powerful Darkness—you will have little or no input into what occurs today. However, Dominion will deal fairly with you. That is, if you cooperate and are willing to accept the mandate outlined for you. If you object, your punishment will be swift and final. Do you understand this mandate?"

There was an awkward silence as each of NO Dom's top brass pondered these words.

"Cypher," Olam said, turning to him. "You are the leader of this force. What is your answer?"

Cypher looked around the table and glanced at each person seated at it. He coughed and then lowered his head. "Yes."

"What do you mean?"

Cypher promptly looked away. "Yes, I understand that I and everyone else in NO Dom must abide by what is set out for us."

"Do you understand the punishments that will follow if you don't abide by the directives of this meeting?"

He cleared his throat. "Yes! I understand that if we don't follow these directives, there'll be a swift and final punishment—for me and all my troops."

Next Olam turned to Cur'sent. "You are NO Dom's Chief of Defence Staff and its main influencer. Do you understand this situation?"

Cur'sent fumbled awkwardly. "Yes… I understand that we must follow the directives of this meeting. And if we don't, there'll be direr consequences."

"I hope you do understand this." Olam turned to Cardinal. "And you? Do you understand this directive?"

Cardinal smiled shyly. "Yes, sir! I fully understand the situation and the consequences of not obeying today's directives."

"Cardinal, you are a persuader. Use your abilities to direct the way ahead wisely."

"Thank you." She smiled. "I will."

Accepting this, Olam turned to the others. "Generals, I've included you in this meeting so you can hear and understand everything that's been said and done. You command the troops and are responsible for their well-being. Do not mislead them. Do you hear what I'm saying to you?"

Each nodded.

"What has occurred is now in the past," Olam continued. "We look to the future and plan for peace. However, we must deal with some things to put this all behind us. First of all, let's discuss the issue of armaments. Cypher, due to your aggressive and self-centred activities, all your armaments will be destroyed."

"If we don't have weapons, how can we protect ourselves?" Cur'sent asked bluntly.

"Due to your aggressive nature, this aspect of the mandate must be strictly followed. If there are any objections, all of your troops will be locked down. All documentation from your headquarters will be removed for evaluation. So are there any objections?"

No one said a word.

"I thought this may be the case," Olam remarked. "Now, here are the rest of my directives. Understand them, as they'll govern you from now on. Cypher, in Dominion you were free to go where you wanted and do as you wanted, when and however you wanted. You chose to be disobedient to the ways of Dominion. Likewise, you were free to do the same in your exile, and yet you again attacked Dominion forces. You call yourself Supreme and Rise Ruler of the so-called New Order Dominion, yet you chose to become Snake, Dragon of Old, the Powerful Darkness. Is this not correct?"

Cypher didn't look up. "Yes…"

"In that case, here are your new directives. You may once again move freely, as you have done. You can go anywhere you want here in Claydonia. But do not enter Dominion proper unless I summon you. Do you agree to this?"

Surprised, they all nodded solemnly.

"If anyone is found outside Claydonia, they'll be imprisoned. Do you hear me?"

There was a chorus of yeses.

"Cypher, when I call you to meet, you must report at the set time," Olam added. "If you fail to report, you will be imprisoned until the time of your punishment. Do you understand?"

"Yes!"

Olam looked at Cypher very intently. "Good. Make sure you don't miss coming, as I don't want to do what I've said I'll do. You may live here as best you can with what you have." He pauses for a moment. "Cypher, in your banishment, and now in your defeat, you and your troops will never again have any power or strength on the battlefield. This means you have been defeated now and forever. And because you have been defeated, I am Light. And I declare that Light will rule all of Dominion and Claydonia. Being Light, I declare, in your defeat, that my integrity stands untarnished. Claydonia will function according to my integrity. I also declare that my good will prevail for the best of all. In Claydonia and Dominion, all will be equal, have their due respect, and receive true, unbiased justice. This is the driving force of my precepts, the governing principles of my agreement. Let it be known that my greatest desire is that everything Dominion stands for will be upheld and adhered to for all of time."

Olam paused to let them think carefully about everything he had said.

Under his breath, though, Cypher suddenly swore. "I'll eliminate that filthy pig..."

Olam heard this. "Cypher? Are you still being defiant?"

"Oh no, sir. I'd never be that defiant."

"Cypher, I've tried many times to help you, and you can change again today, but you are beyond my help. I'll leave you to your troops. I trust that they'll sentence you to your rightful punishment. Because I am who I am, and because I desire freedom for all, I give this freedom to you. I'll not force my ways on you. You're free to do as you choose. But be aware that a time will come when you'll be disciplined for this choice."

Olam took a moment to glance around the table at each person sitting there.

"Now, regarding Claydonia, things are about to change," he continued. "The Claydoms will soon live here as well. And there are several strict limitations you'll have with them. First, you cannot touch them. I mean that you cannot physically touch these Claydoms. Their bodies are off-limits to you. Do you hear what I'm saying?" He paused and then repeated himself firmly. "You cannot touch them!"

Everyone nodded in agreement.

"Make sure you don't touch them physically. If you do, you'll be imprisoned for life." Olam moved on. "This land has been developed and prepared long before you were exiled here. I knew there would eventually be conflict in Dominion, and in fact I planned for you to reside here before the Claydoms came. I waited for you to do what you would do, fulfilling my plans. Know that the Claydoms will live as you do, with the same freedom of choice."

There was a profound silence as all these directives sank in.

"This is all for now," Olam said, wrapping up. "Generals Cha'el and Stren, do you have any remaining items to bring up?"

Cha'el nodded. "We need to set a time for the destruction of the armaments."

"Cypher, what time should this be done?" Olam asked.

Cypher looked uncommitted. "Cur'sent, your thoughts?"

Cur'sent, in turn, looked to the general next to him. "Zez, when?"

"Abb and Brutus?" Zez asked. "When do we destroy our arms?"

Cha'el let out a long sigh. "The arms will be destroyed, and they must be destroyed in the next couple of days! Choose when."

"Cur'sent, it's your decision," said Cypher.

Cur'sent didn't want the responsibility. "Generals, make up your minds."

Before either Zez, Abb, or Brutus could reply, Cha'el lost his patience with them. "Cypher, do you want to destroy them tomorrow or the next day? What will it be?"

"Cursent, which day?" Cypher asked.

"Generals, which day?" Cur'sent asked.

"Will tomorrow work for you, Cypher?" Cha'el asked in disgust.

Frustrated, Cypher swore. "Go ahead. Tomorrow. Destroy them all!" With that, he stood and stumbled over his chair.

"Guards, make him sit down," Stren ordered.

In a flurry of profanity, Cypher grabbed his chair, thumped it down, and sat heavily upon it.

"Cha'el and Stren, destroy the armaments tomorrow," Olam directed.

The two generals of Dominion nodded in understanding.

"There's another issue I wish to raise," said Stren. "Before today's meeting, there were several calls for the immediate execution of General Brutus, as well as Sergeants Tum and Bed. Some also called for the execution of others who have defied orders."

Olam turned to the leader. "Cypher, what is your preference for executing those mentioned?"

Once again, Cypher dodged the question. "Cardinal, what are your thoughts?"

"It doesn't matter to me if they're executed," Cardinal said. "I wouldn't have to deal with their behaviour if they were executed. But they're excellent troops. Brutus is a good general, other than the fact that his violent ways cause problems. Cur'sent, what do you think?"

Cur'sent also passed the buck. "Cypher, you're the commander-in-chief of NO Dom. All executions here fall under your authority."

Cypher looked like he wanted to weasel out of it.

"At this point, it's best to leave all executions for a later date," Olam finally said. "It would be better for them to wait for NO Dom authorities to hold proper trials. Then a review of all facts could be conducted."

No one offered any arguments on this point.

"With these parameters set and agreed upon, let it be resolved that you—Cypher, Cur'sent, and Cardinal—will remain under house arrest until the armaments have been destroyed," Olam said in closing. "At that point, Dominion troops will withdraw from NO Dom. If there is any retaliation during this withdrawal process, the destruction of NO Dom will surely follow. Do you understand?"

Once again, everyone nodded in understanding.

After the leaders of NO Dom had been led out of the meeting tent, Olam stood with his generals and left.

The next day, Dominion's troops began preparations to move out. At 0900 hours that morning, Olam pulled Cha'el aside and instructed him to bring NO Dom leaders out to witness the demolition of the armaments.

By 1000 hours, the first explosion was already rocking the compound. Hours later, once there was nothing left, the troops on both sides watched as the land fell silent.

"Cypher, Cur'sent, and Cardinal, my greatest desire is for you to change your ways," Olam intoned. "But I know your ways. I wish you the best."

Only a day later, Olam and his generals had led all of Dominion's forces away, having marched them back to their landing site on the northwestern coast of Claydonia. As they finally departed, Olam looked forward to the whole business being over. In Dominion, he resolved to hold a week of celebrations every month.

Cypher's Selfishness

Weeks later, Cypher was still licking his emotional wounds from the embarrassment of his defeat and the subsequent disarmament. Thinking about the directives forced upon him led him to unleash vile curses. He felt such humiliation, especially over the matter of executions.

Cur'sent and Cardinal should've dealt with that, he thought to himself. *Instead they dumped it on me.*

He believed that everyone was against him. And when he looked out the window of his office, he saw the generals standing in the parade square below.

No doubt they're talking about me... plotting to take over from me...

"Oh how I despise you, Olam," he murmured aloud. "This is all your fault. If I had known you were going to come here, I never would have done what I have done... why did you sneak around like a worthless pig?"

The sound of soft knocking on his door made him look up.

"Come in," he said, shaking off his self-pity.

Cardinal opened the door. "Excuse me, sir. Could I have a word with you?"

"Yes, of course. Come in. What can I do for you?"

"Sir, if you don't mind, I'm concerned about you…"

"I'm all right."

"Yes, sir. But we haven't talked for a while. Are you upset with Cur'sent and myself?"

Cypher stiffened. "No! Not at all. I've just been busy."

"With all due respect, sir, this has been a horrible time for NO Dom—"

"Yes, I know."

"What I'm saying is that we're all in this together—"

Having caught on, Cypher decided to play the role of the abused leader. "No. I'm fully responsible for everything in NO Dom. Everything stops at the top. I'm at the top."

"With all due respect, sir, many of us issued ordered after Dominion forces landed on our shores. We all agreed to attack. Therefore we're all responsible. And we're all going to put NO Dom back together again."

Cypher didn't like where this was going. He wanted everyone to know that he was still the boss, undisputed.

"No," he said again. "I'm still the final word in NO Dom. I must take responsibility for what's happened."

Cardinal fell silent for a moment and then sidestepped the issue. "Sir, would it be all right if I called a meeting with Cur'sent and the generals so we could discuss… or rather, so you could show us how to make NO Dom great again?"

"If you insist. Would tomorrow be okay?"

"Yes, sir! I'll make arrangements for us to meet at 1000 hours."

With a quick half-salute, Cypher demonstrated that the meeting was over. Cardinal understood that it was time to leave.

As Cardinal gently closed the door, she grimaced. What she really wanted to do was slam the door so hard that it came off its hinges.

"Grow up and get over it," she said under her breath. "With or without you, we've got to get everything back on track here."

She wanted to scream but kept it bottled up.

"You old buzzard… if you don't get a hold of yourself, NO Dom is going to fall apart…"

In his office, though, Cypher continued to fume.

Who does she think she is, coming in here and telling me how to do things? he thought. *I'm still Supreme and Wise Ruler. No one tells me what to do!*

He placed his crown back on and looked north out the window.

A New Strategy

The next day at 0950 hours, the generals crossed the parade square, walking towards headquarters. They weren't in too much of a hurry.

"Things were sure hostile the last time we saw him," Zez remarked.

Abb sighed. "I'm not sure how things will be with the old grouch."

"It would be better for Cur'sent and Cardinal to arrive first," Brutus said. "They could mellow out the battleaxe before we arrive."

Cur'sent diddled along ahead of them.

I hope Cardinal's there first and uses her persuasion to put Cypher in a good mood, the Chief of Defence Staff thought to himself.

If Cypher hated Olam, then Cur'sent equally hated Cypher and In'Mutin. His anger simmered as he thought of them.

Cur'sent was pleased as Cardinal came running up to him, all smiles. She opened the doors and rushed in ahead of all the others.

"Sir!" Cardinal called as she passed Cypher's office. "The troops are on their way and I have some things to discuss before they get here!"

"Come in."

As Cardinal entered, she caught a glimpse of Cypher grabbing the crown and plopping it onto his head.

"Let's meet in the conference room," he said.

She nodded and saluted as they walked down the hall.

"Okay, what have you got?" Cypher said as they sat down around the table.

"First, the common factor for everyone in NO Dom is the belief that we must destroy Olam, our enemy. Once he's gone, there won't be any punishment for us. Second, to get Olam, we must figure out how to influence the Claydoms—"

Just then, the door opened and Cur'sent slowly walked in, interrupting her.

Cur'sent saluted. "Sir!"

The generals came in only a few moments later and took their seats.

"Well, let's begin." Cypher's head snapped up. "We have many matters to deal with! Cardinal, what were you just saying?"

"We need to deal with an item of extreme importance," she said. "Coming to terms with this, we'll be able to change from a defensive posture to an offensive strategy to beat Olam. Listen carefully. We must prepare ourselves."

Cypher looked down at the floor. "Tell us."

"It's about the Claydoms."

Zez seemed surprise. "With all due respect, what about them? They don't have anything to do with us."

"You're wrong. By winning over the Claydoms, we'll increase the number of our forces. Now, I don't know what a

Claydom even is, but we know they're going to have physical bodies. That means we can influence them, even if we can't touch them."

An uneasy fear settled over them. Cypher removed his crown for a moment and felt it in his hands. The feeling sent a shiver through him.

"Physical... something that can be held. Something real..." Suddenly, he slammed his fists on the table and bellowed. "Olam!"

A moment of shock crashed over them.

"We're on our own in this place now," Cypher murmured, consumed by thoughts about everything he had had cheated himself out of, the lies he had told himself, everything that had been taken since the start of his rebellion. He let out a moan. "I wish I'd known."

The others watched him with concern as the darkness around him deepened.

"Yes, we will destroy that filthy, good for nothing pig," their boss said with flaming eyes. "That stinking sewer rat..."

Zez perked up. "Remember, though... Olam told us we are free to go anywhere in Claydonia, once his troops left."

"True," said Cypher. "He also said I'm Supreme and Wise Ruler of NO Dom, that I'm Snake, Dragon of Old, the Powerful Darkness." He held his crown high. "That I am!"

Cur'sent looked around the table. "We will have to change how we perceive ourselves and the world around us."

"And we need to think about the implication of these Claydoms," Cardinal added.

"The implications are major," said Brutus. "We're in charge here. Everyone will be subject to us, including the Claydoms. Is that not so?"

"Yes, the land is ours," Cur'sent agreed. "And we must believe it."

Cypher finally felt like smiling. "Yes, mine. It's Snake's. Snake, Dragon of Old, the Powerful Darkness, has made all this. Olam claims he did, the filthy pig, the incompetent, slimy, lying sewer rat... but the truth is that it was Snake."

"So what's a Claydom?" Cardinal asked. "We must find out what they are, how they think, and how they live so we can, in some way, get them to join us. We need to work out a plan to influence them. That needs to be our strategy."

Abb pondered this further. "Perhaps we will need to change the way we train and indoctrinate our troops."

"How long have we been training the same way?" Brutus growled. "Now you want to change things? I don't see why the old ways aren't good enough."

Cypher snarled at him. "Brute... Snake, Dragon of Old, the Powerful Darkness, will demote you to the lowest ranks in NO Dom if you don't like it. Do you understand me?"

"Yes, sir! It was just a thought."

"Then don't think. Just do what you're told! Snake, Dragon of Old, the Powerful Darkness won't accept any disagreement."

Brutus bit his lip and suppressed his anger. "Yes, sir."

An awkward silence fell over the conference room.

"In everything we do, our strategy must be to win over these Claydoms so they don't know what's happened," Cardinal said. "Then, as our numbers grow, we'll have the personnel to win over Olam and retake Dominion."

Suddenly, Cypher jumped up. "Okay, let's get to it. We're going to influence the Claydoms to join us! It was foolish of Olam to commit to bringing the Claydoms here. We've got him now."

Called to Dominion

It wasn't long before Cypher finally heard from Olam. The commander-in-chief of Dominion wanted Cypher to report to his office in Dominion the following Wednesday at 1000 hours.

On getting this order, Cypher flew into a panic, cursing and swearing. He ripped off his crown, plopped it on his desk, and rushed out of his office to inform Cur'sent and Cardinal of this latest development.

"I wonder what he wants with you?" Cardinal asked.

"I don't know," Cypher said, feeling guilty. "I haven't done anything, and the Claydoms aren't here yet. All we've done is talk about them."

Cur'sent sighed. "Well, you'll have to go deal with this."

"What should I tell him?"

"That's your detail to work out," Cur'sent said. "Now go! Stop fretting! You're driving us crazy."

But Cypher couldn't help but fret. What would Olam want to talk with him about? What would he be asked? How should he answer?

When he arrived at Olam's office, the administrator at the front desk smiled happily and welcomed Cypher.

Oh sure, Cypher thought. *You're all smiles, but you're not the one meeting Olam…*

As Cypher entered, Olam stood up. "Hello, Cypher. Please be seated."

Cypher restlessly sat.

"How are you doing, Cypher?"

"Ah… okay."

"What have you been doing?" Olam asked, even though he already knew.

"Not much. Just going here and there, seeing what's happening in Claydonia."

"Good! What do you think of the northern lake with the waterfalls?"

Cypher squirmed. "I haven't been there yet."

"Oh? It's near your headquarters. You can see it from the window on the north side of your office…" Olam then changed the subject. "What I want to talk to you about are the Claydoms."

"Ah. What do you want to know? As far as I know, they haven't come yet. And I certainly haven't touched them."

"I want you to understand something about them, Cypher."

Cypher felt bewildered that Olam would have invited him here to give him any information about the Claydoms.

"Cypher, there's an immense difference between the nature of the Claydoms and the nature of who we are, you and me. You and me are spirits. The Claydoms combine a spirit nature with something physical. As you know, Claydonia itself is physical. The physical elements of that place will have a distinct effect on the Claydoms that they don't have on you."

"Excuse me, sir, but why would it affect them and not us?"

"As I've said, you're not physical. They are." Olam leaned back in his seat. "You cannot really control the physical realm, you know. You can use the physical for your benefit. I've established the physical world to operate by certain physical laws. Only I can change the physical, since I'm the one who made it."

Cypher looked down at the floor. "But Snake, Dragon of Old, the Powerful Darkness…"

"You know full well that you don't have that authority. In fact, you have no authority over the physical whatsoever." Olam spoke very firmly. "Cypher, do you understand me?"

"Yes, sir," Cypher replied without looking up.

"Remember, as I've told you, that you are not in any way to touch the Claydoms physically. Is this not correct?"

"Yes, sir. I remember."

"Cypher, I know you'll try to influence them. When it comes to freedom of choice, I've given them the same privileges as you and the rest of Dominion. It's what I believe. It's how Dominion functions. They are free to do whatever they want, whenever they want, wherever they want, however they want, with whoever they want. They're the only ones who choose what they do in life. The same as with you."

With this, Cypher sat up straighter. "Yes, sir!"

"I also need to remind you that I won't lie to them, nor will I steal from them, nor will I cheat them out of anything to gain their influence," Olam said. "You know that I stand as Truth. I'll lead Claydoms with true justice, as I do here in Dominion. I will continue to do the best for all, no matter the costs. This is who I am. You also know that when the time comes, there'll be consequences for what you've chosen. If any Claydom decides to go with you, they'll receive the same punishment you and your troops will receive. Do you understand what I've said to you?"

Cypher suddenly felt a renewed sense of defiance. "Yes, sir! You've said that I'm free to do whatever I want, wherever I want, whenever I want, however I want, and with whoever I want!"

Olam stood up. "You've always been defiant. You will receive the punishment you've chosen. It's best you leave now."

Once Cypher left, Olam sat back down in his seat. He felt heavy-hearted knowing the events that were to come.

But this is the only way I'll know whether they're truly for me, he reminded himself. *No matter what, I must leave the choice to them.*

Getting to Work

After rushing back to Claydonia, Cypher called Cur'sent and Cardinal to his office. While waiting, he rubbed his hands together and paced back and forth.

"What took you so long?" he barked when his top brass hurried through the door. He smiled and laughed sinisterly. "Sit down!"

Cur'sent and Cardinal looked at each other uncertainly as their boss began to explain with sinister glee.

"What a day this is," Cypher mused. "Oh yes. What a day! Yes! You should've been there as I met with that old scoundrel. I told Olam exactly what I'm going to do, and he can't do anything about it."

Cypher reached for his crown. He placed it on his head.

"I told him. Yeah, I told him. I'm now in charge of this place! Yes. I told that old good for nothing filthy pig that it doesn't matter what he says. No, I'm in charge here. I'm free to do whatever I want, wherever I want, whenever I want, however I want, and with whoever I want! And he can't stop me."

He walked over to the window and looked out to the north. Sure enough, there was a beautiful lake in that direction with a magnificent waterfall.

"You know, I've never seen that before," he said. "I wonder how it got there…"

Cur'sent and Cardinal stood up to leave, but Cypher saw their reflection in the glass and snapped at them.

"Where do you think you're going?"

Cur'sent felt startled. "We thought you were done."

"I'm not done until I'm *done*." Cypher glared at them. "From now on, things will be different. You know what Olam's doing, right? He's sending the Claydoms here—"

"We know this," Cardinal ventured uncertainly.

"Don't interrupt me! Besides, you don't know. They'll be like us, and they'll be physical!"

"What do you mean, physical?" Cur'sent asked with a frown.

"They'll be able to choose. Yes, choose. Just as we can. I've got Olam now. He says that he made them with the freedom to choose, to speak and go and do whatever they want. You know what this means? They can choose him… or they can choose *me*."

Cypher turned abruptly to Cardinal. "What's your take on this, Cardinal?"

She didn't know what to say, but she gave him a fiery glare.

"Oh, come on." Cypher waved his hand dismissively. "I didn't mean to anger you with such an important question. Maybe go and take some time to think about it."

Cardinal jumped to her feet. "You're a ranting, raving, demanding lunatic. What's gotten under your stupid crown? Who do you think you are anyway?"

"Cypher, you need to smarten up," Cur'sent added, steaming. "We're the only thing standing between you and the forces. So don't push it. All we need to do is say you're gone, and you're gone!"

Cypher continued to wave them off. "Oh, come on now. I didn't mean what I said. I was just excited about my meeting with Olam... I guess I got a bit carried away."

Cur'sent glowered at the boss. "Don't get carried away like that again, Cypher, or you'll be the one who gets carried off."

Cypher ducked the threat. "Yes. Let's put this behind us."

"That said, we do need our generals to develop a strategy to influence the Claydoms," Cardinal said. "That's the first step."

"I should apologize for my rant," Cypher said, sounding more compassionate than usual. "But there's truth in what I said."

A few moments of peace followed. Everything seemed to have been set aright between the three leaders of NO Dom.

"Would you two schedule a meeting with the generals?" Cypher asked.

Cur'sent saluted. "Yes, sir!"

Once he was alone, Cypher slapped his desk angrily. "I'll eliminate both of those useless idiots when I'm done with them. They'll wish they'd never contradicted me..."

But as Cur'sent and Cardinal walked down the hallway together, they muttered about what they'd just witnessed.

"That old buzzard just about lost his head," Cardinal said.

Cur'sent rolled his eyes in disgust. "More than just his fat head!"

Together they began to outline a new military strategy. With his egotism, Cur'sent knew what would be needed to control the Claydoms. With her gift of persuasion, Cardinal knew exactly how to approach them. It would look like they were doing the best for the Claydoms. They would never know they were being controlled.

The Claydoms

Excited, Olam chose the first two handsome and beautiful Claydoms to which all the others would be born. They were intelligent, enthusiastic, diligent, good-natured, humorous, and healthy.

Upon their arrival at Claydonia, Olam introduced them to their home. They were excited to see the beauty surrounding them.

"All this is for you," Olam said. "I've supplied everything you need for your lives and the generations to come. Use it wisely. Living here is your privilege. You're free to do whatever you want, whenever you want, wherever you want, however you want, with whoever you want. This freedom to choose is yours There's only one thing I ask. There's a fragrant yellow flower growing beside a sparkling lake. It's far beyond the hills, and it's fed by a waterfall. This lovely yellow flower grows only at the bottom of that waterfall. I'm asking that you don't pick or smell this flower. When you pick or smell it, a change will come over you, revealing that which is good and not for you. Do you understand?"

Both of the Claydoms agreed.

"This then is an agreement between us."

Olam spent much time with this couple, and one day he asked them to give themselves names. Several more days passed before he followed up with them about what they had decided.

The man excitedly gestured to the woman. "She is Twilight, because she's the beginning of life here in Claydonia."

Twilight smiled. "The best name for him is Kindle, because together we have kindled life here in Claydonia."

"You've chosen beautiful names," Olam said, feeling pleased. "Kindle and Twilight, I've made you free to choose. However, I've also assigned acquaintances for you. They're here to help you."

"What are they like?" Kindle asked.

"These acquaintances are available at your request. If you would like their help, you must ask. They'll gladly help you. Their names are Ly'Bar, Shrew, Fi'Denc, Bo'wabel, Be'soth, Acc'Plish, Fre'Dobe, Tu, Teg, Shi'lid, Pas'on, Jus'ten, Oth'kin, O'bed, and In'Mutin."

General Abb's surveillance unit was hidden in the woods nearby, watching and listening to this exchange between Olam and the new Claydoms. He was taken aback by what he witnessed.

As soon as Abb sent a dispatch back to headquarters, they reported to Cardinal. Cardinal, in turn, only dispatched to Cypher the details that she felt he needed to know.

What Olam had told Kindle and Twilight about the acquaintances aroused in them a captivating desire. They yearned to find one of these new acquaintances.

One day, while the couple was sitting and talking beside a beautiful creek, Ly'Bar came to them. They were so excited to meet him!

"How are you?" asked Twilight.

"I'm great!" Ly'Bar hesitated for a moment. "I'd like to get to know you two."

"We'd like that," said Kindle. "What's your name?"

After they had all introduced themselves, Ly'Bar made an offer. "If you want, I'd like to help you discover all the amazing things Chief Olam has prepared for you."

Time passed quickly for the couple as Ly'Bar aided them in exploring their new home and gaining knowledge of it. He helped them discover how to have fun and how to enjoy being with one another. Together they built a shelter and found foods they liked. They even learned about the animals and many different plants that grew nearby.

Angry Again

"Cur'sent, it's been a long time since Cypher last requested a parade and celebration," Cardinal mused one day while they were at work together at headquarters. "The troops need to have something to look forward to, and I think an update on the Claydoms would inspire them."

The prospect excited Cur'sent. "There's been some discrepancies in the various reports we've gotten about the Claydoms. Let's go to Abb to verify what's actually going on. Maybe we can see them for ourselves."

It didn't take long to organize a tour of the land where the Claydoms had made their home. Cypher, Cur'sent, and Cardinal paid close attention as Abb walked them through the sights, briefing them on all that had occurred here so far. It seemed that the Claydoms were so far unaware that they were being observed.

Cypher, Cur'sent, and Cardinal were awed at seeing the Claydoms for the first time. What a creature they were! Handsome and beautiful. Their talking and laughter surprised their observers. The excitement in their voices resonated through the trees.

"Why are they so happy?" Cardinal asked in pure delight.

Cur'sent was bewildered. "They're all by themselves… why are they so excited?"

"They're happy about being alive," Cypher said, stunned. "And everything is so bright here!"

Abb smiled. "Yes! The light is warm and inviting. It's peaceful."

The beauty of this land struck Cur'sent, who was still scarred by the devastation of the recent war. "Everything is so new. All the trees and plants are growing"

"Yes," Cypher said, nodding. "And why are all the animals so content?"

"Do you notice that pleasing aroma?" Cardinal said. "It sends a shiver of excitement through me like I've never felt before."

They all stood in awe of the beauty and peace before them.

"Would you like to see more?" Abb asked.

Cypher, whose countenance had changed from happiness to resentment, suddenly snapped. "I've seen enough. Oh how I hate Olam!" Once again, his anger consumed him. He waved his hand over the scene before him. "He gives these… these *Claydom* all this while we're stuck in a dark, stinking hole!"

He turned his back on them and began to stalk away.

"Get me out of here. Now." Cypher picked up his pace. Roaring, he demanded, "Get me back to headquarters! I'll destroy Olam for this…"

Cur'sent's anger also exploded. He grabbed Cypher, threw him to the ground, and piled on him with his fist, ready to dispatch him. The only thing that stopped him was Cardinal, who jumped in and prevented him from finishing their boss.

"Cypher!" In burning anger, Cur'sent stood up. "I told you never again to lose it, or your head would roll. Your anger doesn't help anything! Sure, go ahead and hate Olam! I hate him too. But to beat him, we'll need to have cool heads. And we need to get these Claydoms on our side."

Cardinal was angry too and turned on Cypher. "If we don't get together as a united force, we won't succeed. So what do you want? Do you want to fight it out right now with Cur'sent and me? Or do you want to cool down, get a different attitude, return to headquarters, and solve this problem?"

On their way back, Cypher finally settled down. By the time they got back to his office, he was merely agitated.

The following day, Cypher still hadn't left his office and Cur'sent and Cardinal were growing increasingly disgusted with him.

Finally, they decided to knock on his door. When they did, In'Mutin slipped out and walked away. Then Cypher invited them inside. He was back at the window, staring out at the waterfalls in the distance.

"What's the plan?" Cur'sent asked.

Cypher turned to face them. "Okay, we need to get something straight. I'm Supreme and Wise Ruler of NO Dom."

Cardinal sat down, feeling annoyed. "Then act like it!"

"Overnight I've decided to control my anger and focus on taking Olam out," Cypher assured them.

"I'll put everything behind us if you can keep focused on that goal," Cur'sent said. "But if you don't stay focused on Olam, you won't like the result."

"I'm giving you my word." Cypher changed the subject. "How are the plans coming along to retrain our troops?"

Cardinal sighed. "We've got a rough draft and are still filling in the details."

"Good. Keep at it." Cypher glanced at the window again. "I believe I have some time to get it right. First off, I'll hold another meeting with the generals. Next Thursday at 0900 hours? We'll parade next week."

The officers stood to leave.

"Thank you for getting my attention focused on what really matters," Cypher said.

"You're welcome," said Cur'sent.

With that, they saluted and left.

Misgivings

Over the weeks, Kindle and Twilight enjoyed discovering new things about their environment that satisfied their curiosity. They also resolved with Ly'Bar to focus on new acquaintances.

Fi'Denc was a cheery gal who was so confident that she gave the Claydoms immense pleasure in their mutual discoveries. Not only did they ask Fi'Denc to help, but they also asked Tu, with the help of Ly'Bar, to determine the exact meaning behind their new discoveries.

Every evening, the couple had a deeper resolve to discover even more about their new lives. But they still had questions.

"Kindle, it's been an excited time of discovery, but I don't understand this strange feeling inside me," Twilight said to her mate.

"I'm struggling with the same strange feelings."

Twilight turned to their closest acquaintance. "Ly'Bar, I have this strong feeling that I want to do the best for Kindle. What is it?"

"I've seen it in you both," said Ly'Bar. "This is Be'soth at work."

Be'soth soon arrived to explain the phenomenon—sort of. "If you want to understand me, you need Fre'Dobe and Shi'lid to walk with you," he said.

They were still trying to figure out their confusing feelings when Olam appeared. The chief noticed their questioning looks at once.

"What are you thinking?" Olam asked.

"We're wondering about this strange feeling inside us."

Olam smiled. "It comes from Be'soth. Allow him to become the driving force in you. Do as he directs and you'll live a good life." Seeing their confusion, Olam continued. "Spend time with Be'soth. Enjoy him. As you follow him, Shi'lid will flow from you, and you'll experience a deep connection with Pas'on. As Pas'on fills you to overflowing, you'll never be able to hold it in."

They walked together to the creek, where Olam sat down. Twilight and Kindle got down and sat on either side of him. Olam tried to help them further understand the nature of Be'soth and the other acquaintances.

"As you better understand Be'soth, you'll also meet the acquaintances who support you. There's Jus'ten, Tu, and Teg. Follow O'bed's instructions. And as Acc'Plish develops, hold tight to Teg. With Teg comes the support from Oth'kin and Jus'ten. As these acquaintances spend time with you, it will be the same as if they are with me."

The couple looks over and saw Shi'lid and Be'soth lying nearby on the soft grass, also pondering what Olam had said.

"I enjoy being with you," Olam said contently, taking in their gentle laughter. "I appreciate you and your potential. I love you immensely."

Weeks later, Ly'Bar once again joined the Claydom couple by the creek where they liked to visit.

"Where would you like to explore?" asked the acquaintance.

"How about the hills?" Twilight said, feeling a twinge of misgivings stir in her. "Or the lake and the waterfalls…"

"Okay," said Ly'Bar. "Let's go!"

The hills had seemed like they were just beyond the trees, but along the way they discovered gentle valleys and rugged gorges. And everywhere they went, they breathed in the fresh, cool air.

As they approached the top of the waterfalls, Twilight marvelled at all the beauty around them.

"Look, Kindle!" she said. "What a view. It's beautiful…"

But when she looked over the edge of the falls, at the water crashing down onto the rocks below, she felt a little bit scared.

As the sun sank into the west, Be'soth nudged Kindle into realizing the time.

"Twilight, let's go," Kindle said. "It'll be late when we get back to our lodge."

With the moon and stars shining down on them, they reminisced about the day.

"Kindle, that's the greatest things we've discovered so far," Twilight said. "I'll never forget the power of the waterfalls and shimmering lake. What a sensation!"

Kindle looked unsettled. "But I have a strange, haunted feeling."

"I don't understand this uncertainty."

"I've felt a kind of foreboding. It's stirring feelings of apprehension." He held Twilight tight. "I don't know what it means, but it's troubling."

The Waterfalls

After a restless night, Ly'Bar awakened the couple.

"Come on," he said. "Let's go back to the lake and waterfall and see the flowers."

"I'd strongly suggest not going there." O'bed cautioned them.

"What about going to see those flowers?" Ly'Bar asked the couple as they walked through the wilderness. "Are you two sure they're there? The only way to find out is to look."

"That's right," said In'Mutin. "Just a look won't hurt."

"Let them decide," O'bed advised In'Mutin.

In'Mutin didn't agree. "Twilight and Kindle you'll forget if you wait too long. I say you should go there and find out the truth."

He wasn't the only one to think so.

"Twilight and Kindle, if you want to put this to rest, you should go and look," agreed Shrew. "Besides, you're not getting any younger."

"You're tired from yesterday's long hike," said Shi'lid. "Why not go swimming, relax, have something to eat, and then have a good night's rest. Tomorrow you'll be rested and be able to think more clearly."

Together, Kindle and Twilight decided to put it off by one more day.

The next day, though, Kindle and Twilight slept in. Ly'Bar felt very frustrated by them.

"Okay, it looks like today is another day of rest," Ly'Bar remarked. "Maybe we can go look at the flowers tomorrow."

"Give them time to figure this out," said Jus'ten. "There's no hurry!"

However, Ly'Bar felt very impatient. "Either they'll find out the truth about the flowers or they'll get busy with life and never again find the time."

"They have the freedom to choose," Be'soth reminded them. "So let them choose."

Tu thought so, too. "I'm with Be'soth. You should instead have a feast. Then go for a walk, swim, and rest."

The following morning, all the acquaintances were waiting for Kindle and Twilight as they awakened in the lodge. Bright-eyed, Kindle was excited to go looking for an easy path to the waterfalls.

"We'll go south to the aspens, then head southeast to the bend in the river," said Kindle. "Once there, we'll be able to see the best way to follow."

Surprised by his initiative, the acquaintances all cheerfully decided to go with him and Twilight.

It didn't take long for them to reach the river bend.

"Let's follow this game trail along the river," Kindle suggested.

When they came into view of the waterfalls, Twilight was amazed by the sight of them, as well as the fresh, moist air.

They decided to follow the river until it turned its flow southwest.

"Look at the lake!" marveled Twilight as they got closer.

The lake's water was rippling in the breeze under the bright sun. But there were dark, billowing clouds forming in the east.

Scared, Twilight suggested that they return to the lodge.

"Why let some clouds stop you?" Ly'Bar urged. "You're almost there."

O'bed frowned at his fellow acquaintance. "Ly'Bar, let them decide."

"But if you don't tell them what to do, they won't do it," In'Mutin said.

"In'Mutin!" O'bed was aghast. "Chief Olam made them free to choose. So let them choose!"

Ly'Bar shook his head. "The flowers will fade. Then their real aroma will be gone. Besides, Acc'Plish will be thrilled that you made it to the falls. That aroma will stay with you for the rest of your life."

Twilight seemed intrigued by the suggestion.

"Why not find out what they smell like?" In'Mutin asked her.

O'bed was growing increasingly alarmed. "You know what Chief Olam said about the flowers…"

Fi'Denc recited the warning: "Be careful. Something will change in you."

"Make sure of the truth before you do this," Tu whispered to Twilight.

But Twilight was now walking with singular purpose. "Kindle, let's get closer. I want to see those flowers before we return to the lodge tonight."

"That's the best choice you could make," said In'Mutin.

All the while, a threatening darkness was arising from the east and moving towards them as they approached the bottom of the falls.

Chief Olam and his generals watched the Claydoms from their lookout at the top of the waterfalls, concealed by the darkness encroaching from the east.

"Generals, this is a tough time," he said, crossing his arms. "I must not interfere with their decision. It's theirs."

Cypher and his top commanders were also waiting nearby, leaning as close as they could to witness the event. Abb had informed them that the Claydoms were on their way to the waterfalls, and Cypher had acted quickly. This would be the perfect opportunity to begin influencing them.

He just didn't want to get close enough to accidentally alarm Olam.

"This is a great day for NO Dom," he said to himself as he approached alongside Cur'sent and Cardinal. "I am Snake, Dragon of Old, the Powerful Darkness."

"You can do this," encouraged Cur'sent. "I'll be with you. From now on, these Claydoms will be ours."

"Whatever you say, make them doubt Olam," Cardinal advised. "Doubt is the greatest tactic in persuasion."

As they watched, Cypher disguised himself as Snake and moved slowly towards the unsuspecting couple.

Kindle and Twilight were absorbed by the water, watching as it splashed over the rocks. They felt exhilarated, captivated by the sun's warmth and cool spray of the falls.

"Kindle!" Twilight called to her mate. "Look at these beautiful flowers! Aren't they just gorgeous?"

Sensing her immense joy, he leaned into her hug. In awe, they gazed together at the beautiful yellow flowers.

Suddenly, a warm and seductive voice spoke. Looking around, they realized that the brightness of the day had faded. Darkness from the east had fallen over them.

"Did Chief Olam say you're not to smell the flowers?" the voice asked.

"Chief Olam said we're not to pick this one," Kindle answered. "If we do, a change will come over us."

Twilight gasped as she saw the source of the voice: a snake slithering towards them through the grass.

"You won't change," Snake hissed seductively. "When you smell the flowers, you'll know within you what is good and what isn't."

A battle was now raging within the two Claydoms.

"Olam asked you not to pick or smell these flowers," O'bed reminded them. "You've seen them for yourself. Now go! Go back to your lodge."

In'Mutin leaned in close. "O'bed, leave them alone!"

But the Claydoms seems to agree that it was a good idea to pick the flowers and smell them. They wanted to find out what was good and what wasn't.

So together they picked one of the yellow flowers and brought it to their noses. The flower's scent surged through them, and with it came the realization of their physical existence. It struck them like an ice-cold wind.

Kindle and Twilight, realizing their physical condition, rushed to their lodge to find something to cover themselves.

On their way, In'Mutin shouted to them gleefully. "Congratulations! You now know. You can choose what's good and what's not. It's your choice!"

After the deed, Cypher slithered off and transformed back into his true self. Along with Cur'sent and Cardinal, he scrambled back to his headquarters.

"They're mine!" crowed Cypher in elation once they were back in his office. "I now control those Claydoms. You were right, Cardinal. Doubt works. They're mine! All mine! Let's celebrate our win! Cur'sent and Cardinal, call our generals to celebrate this momentous day."

Confronted

Olam was waiting for Kindle and Twilight when they arrived at the lodge. Seeing Olam, they were afraid of him.

"Where've you been?" Olam asked them. "Why the hurry to get inside?"

Kindle avoided him. "We've been to the waterfalls."

"It's dark and we're cold," Twilight said with tears in her eyes. "We need something to cover ourselves with."

Olam's voice became grave. "Have you picked a flower and smelled it?"

"Yes," Kindle admitted.

"I told you that something would change in you when you picked the flower and smelled it. Is this not the truth?" Olam sighed. "You're cold and want to be covered because you've changed. You didn't trust me and chose to disregard our agreement. You've been disobedient. Before you picked and smelled the flowers, you were spirit-oriented and part of Dominion. Now you've become physically-oriented, focused on yourself rather than being a free spirit. From now on, you'll be focused on yourselves and what you can get."

At the top of the waterfalls, Olam instructed his generals to get Cypher and bring him to the Claydoms' lodge. When this was done, Cypher cowered before the commander-in-chief.

"Cypher, you are now without any appeal. You are condemned to your final punishment. You'll no longer be known as Cypher, the tall, handsome, brilliant one who shone as a great leader. You'll now be known for the symbol you've chosen: a snake. You'll crawl on your belly."

With this pronouncement, Dominion's generals released Cypher. As he fell to the ground, he turned into a snake once again and slithered away.

"Olam! I'll get you for this!" he yelled.

Their task done, Olam and his generals returned to Dominion.

Having overheard everything that had happened, Cur'sent and Cardinal followed Cypher to where he had slithered.

"Get me back to headquarters," Cypher yelled in frustration.

"You got yourself into this," Cur'sent replied angrily. "Get yourself out!"

Cardinal and Cur'sent turned and began walking away, leaving Cypher alone in the tall grass.

"Cur'sent! Cardinal! Don't leave!" Cypher tried taking on a gentler tone of voice. "I apologize for my outrage. It's because I can't walk…"

"Snake, hear me," Cur'sent called back. "You've been condemned to crawl for the rest of your life. We're not!"

Remorse

Seeing Cypher slither away, the Claydoms quickly went into their lodge. They spent a long, cold, sleepless night as the day's events raced through their minds. They awakened several times to talk about what had happened. Kindle tried to settle Twilight as she burst into deep, unresolvable crying. He got choked up, too, with tears of realization trickling down his cheeks.

"We should've left the falls and not picked the flower," he resolved.

"I wish we'd never gone to the falls to see the flowers," she agreed. "We should've listened and trusted Chief Olam and our acquaintances."

Kindle clouded over with anger. "Why didn't Ly'Bar, In'Mutin, or Shrew warn us?"

"Why'd Chief Olam make us? Why'd he bring us here?" Twilight wondered. "He should've known what we were going to do! Why didn't he stop us? If he'd stopped us, we wouldn't have picked that flower. It's all his fault!"

They wallowed in self-pity, and eventually they fell into the most heated and hateful argument they'd ever had. Yelling at each other, they blamed the other for not doing something, or for doing the wrong thing. They rolled over in bed and stared at the walls, muttering about the other.

As they fretted and fumed, they sank into a fitful sleep.

And when the morning came, they continued to wallow in how badly they had been treated by the other. They clumsily got ready for the day without speaking and stumbled out of their lodge to get out of there.

They were soon joined by Cur'sent and Cardinal. The Claydoms didn't recognize them but soon accepted them as a pair of new acquaintances.

"How are you doing?" Cur'sent asked with a smirk. "You know, just being neighbourly."

Twilight exploded at him. "If you'd gone through what I've gone through, you wouldn't be asking!"

Cur'sent smiled to himself. *Wow! Do we ever have them now…*

The Claydoms went on for some time, complaining about Olam and their acquaintances who had all failed to stop them from making their bad decision.

"If Olam really cared for you, he should've stopped you from picking those flowers," Cardinal said. "And if your acquaintances are who they say they are, they should have stopped you. They're spineless. Who do they think they are anyway?"

Cur'sent pressed the point home. "Your friend In'Mutin gave you the best direction. The choice was yours. He didn't just stand there! He told you what you had to do. I'd trust him before I'd ever trust Olam. He was with you. Olam wasn't!"

When the pair had settled down, Cur'sent and Cardinal chose to separate them and talk to them individually. Cur'sent pulled Kindle aside while Cardinal went over to talk with Twilight.

Twilight burst into tears. "I might as well just leave this place…"

Cardinal, knowing that Twilight was pregnant and that she and her forces would need all the Claydoms they could get if they wanted to fight Olam, responded warmly.

"My dear, I'm your friend," Cardinal said. "Trust me! You've had a bad night. But it was only one night. Things will get better."

"Are you sure? I sure hope so, because I'm not going through another night like that one."

Cardinal nodded. "Twilight, I'm your friend. If you need any help, you can come to me."

"Chief Olam said we're to ask him."

Hearing Olam's name, Cardinal's anger flared. "Listen to me. I know the best for you. I'm here with you right now. He isn't!"

Something inside Twilight felt uneasy, but she went along with it.

After this conversation, she went back to the lodge to find Kindle. Despite their disagreement during the night, she felt reassured by his presence at her side.

The same was true of him, for he sighed in relief when he saw her.

"What a relief," he said to her, eyeing Cur'sent and Cardinal as they wandered away. "You know, now that they're gone it feels as though something heavy's been lifted from me."

"What just happened wasn't right or good," Twilight added. "Everything feels wrong. It makes me feel violated."

Suddenly, Twilight heard Be'soth's voice whispering to her: "Twilight, let Kindle know you're no longer upset with him…"

She realized that the acquaintance was right. "Kindle, I'm sorry! I love you very much. I've said things I shouldn't have."

With tears flowing down their cheeks, Kindle hugged her. "So did I! I love you, too Would you forgive me?"

New Leadership

After visiting the Claydoms, Cur'sent and Cardinal rejoined Snake as he continued his slow crawl towards headquarters.

"I don't want any of the staff or troops to see me like this," Snake warned. "I'll eventually be able to meet with the generals from behind my desk. Hopefully, they'll focus on my crown. As for parades and official function, you two can handle those. You can inform our soldiers that Olam's generals captured me. I was badly injured trying to escape and can't walk."

They agreed that this would work.

Cur'sent and Cardinal called the generals to a meeting.

"A couple of days ago, Olam's generals seized Snake out of NO Dom headquarters," Cur'sent informed them. "He's been badly injured and will no longer take part in parades. In fact, from now on, our Supreme and Wise Ruler, Cypher, will be known exclusively as Snake, Dragon of Old, the Powerful Darkness."

Cardinal cut in. "He's well enough to do his job. However, he can only meet with you in his office."

"Can we see him now?" asked General Zez.

"Not at present," Cur'sent replied. "If you can give him a few weeks to recover, we'll make arrangements to meet with him again. In the meantime, Snake has asked Cardinal and me to provide all necessary leadership."

The generals clearly had many questions, but Cur'sent put his hand up to avoid answering them. Instead the generals saluted and quietly left the conference room.

"Zez, I'm confused about how Snake would be captured like that without any of us finding out about it," said General Brutus in confusion. "The story is suspicious…"

OLAM'S VISIT

Now that Kindle and Twilight had a little one on the way, they needed to get ready to have a family. One day, feeling content, they walked down to the creek, where they swam and gathered food before returning to the lodge.

As the day cooled, Olam greeted them.

"I've brought you something to cover yourselves," he said. "I want to help you understand what has just occurred. I've said you are free to choose, and you will continue to choose your way. From now on, you'll be focused on yourselves and what you can get rather than being a free spirit. In the meantime, I'd encourage you to understand your acquaintances and how they affect your choices."

Olam continued with a detailed explanation to answer the many questions that had recently occurred to the Claydoms.

"By now you've met Cur'sent and Cardinal. Be aware of who they are and their influence over what you choose. As for the flower, know that it's only a plant. It has no value other than being beautiful and having an attractive aroma. But symbolically, it attracted your curiosity. This attraction was meant to lay bare your true desires. When you picked the flower, it revealed that you didn't trust me. Rather, you trusted yourselves. And doing what you wanted rather than doing what I asked reveals that you've listened to In'Mutin. This mutiny is an act of disobedience that brings guilt. When you made this choice, you brought upon yourselves, and all future Claydoms, the curse of selfish disobedience. It's Cur'sent's true character revealed. Be aware of the ways of those like Cur'sent and In'Mutin. They are bent on selfishness and self-gratification. All Claydoms will also bear this curse of self-centeredness. The curse will hold you captive in your physical forms."

"But what of Cardinal?" Twilight asked.

"Cardinal is that which persuades. She is the founding lie that promotes and permits all other lies, the one who manipulates, distorts, and misleads to promote and encourages selfish disobedience. She is anything and everything that persuades you or others what to believe and do. She is strongly influenced by Cur'sent and In'Mutin. Her ways are all about self-preservation. She will promote anything to persuade you that the truth is a lie and the lie is the truth."

Kindle nodded, taking this in.

"Remember your acquaintances. Learn to listen to them," Olam continued. "I wish you well in the life you've chosen. You'll no longer see the spirit world, but never forget that you are free to choose. Choose wisely. I'll talk with you whenever you want—and when you'd like to rejoin Dominion, we'll talk."

The couple then watched, sadly, as Olam departed.

Something about his appearance to them that day made them feel both gratified and afraid at the same time. They realized they were feeling the same thing.

"I don't know what tomorrow will bring," Twilight said. "Or what will become of our child."

Kindle agreed. "I appreciate Chief Olam's help, but it seems he has left the future unknown. We'll have to figure it out as we go."

"That scares me! Because I don't know what we'll choose. I don't know if our choices will benefit us…"

The following day, while walking through the forest around the lodge, Twilight was joined by several of the acquaintances.

"I'm not sure we have enough food here for ourselves and our future kids," Twilight mused as she looked around at the trees. "Ever since what happened at the waterfalls, I've an awkward feeling about this place."

Now that their lives had changed, Twilight was realizing that everything would be different than it had been.

"I've noticed that it's been getting darker here," Kindle said. "I don't like it. I think we should go to the northwest. The sky seems brighter."

When Kindle suggested this, they agreed to explore that area. The main reason they had built the first lodge on this ground was that Olam had brough them there.

"Let's find a grassy spot with lots of room for the kids to play," Twilight suggested.

Kindle smiled. "Yes. A place protected from the wind and storms. After all, Chief Olam told us we can choose whatever we want."

They began their search immediately, and before long they came to a beautiful, bright valley. Twilight held Kindle's hand as they gazed in amazement at the scenery. Peace flowed through them.

"Kindle, this is it," Twilight said tearfully. "Would you be okay if we built a new home here? If it isn't right, we can keep looking. Whatever we choose, I want you to like it as well."

Kindle's eyes were wide. "Thank you, but this place is magnificent."

Having made their decision, they returned to their old lodge to excitedly pack all their possessions and take them to their new home.

Sinister Plot

It was late in the day when Cur'sent and Cardinal walked back to Snake's office and knocked on the door.

"How did your meeting go with my generals?" Snake asked.

Cardinal shrugged. "Better than I thought."

"We put them off for a few weeks to get things together here," Cur'sent added. "They want to talk to you soon to get your input."

Snake growled. "Why do they need me to tell them what happened? You've already told them."

"We've been thinking that we need to do something different," Cardinal said after a few moments had passed. "We've come to get your insights."

"Sure. Now you ask my insight," Snake muttered. "You never did before!"

Cur'sent cleared his throat. "From our reports, it seems that the Claydoms are looking to move—"

Snake had no patience for this. "In controlling the Claydoms, I must show them my great value…"

"That'll be easy," Cur'sent reasoned. "They've been disobedient to Olam."

"We have plenty of time to develop our war plan." Cardinal raised her eyebrows. "As you know, they are beginning to multiply now. We must train our forces to influence their descendants so they proclaim our truth: that there's no one like you, Snake."

Snake beamed with pride. "Exactly."

"Under my control, I'll amaze the Claydoms of Claydonia with my powers."

"What do you think about placing my image as an emblem on everything I own?" Snake asked.

Cardinal was pleased with this idea. "Good. We'll have statues made of you, so the Claydoms see you often and ascribe immense value to you."

Snake leaned back and looked out the window at the waterfalls again. "Olam, you filthy pig. You're done. We've got your precious Claydoms."

Next they turned their attention back to the original declaration Cypher had made about Snake. It took a few moments to locate the document:

> Snake, Dragon of Old, the Powerful Darkness is eternal. Snake has been, is, and will always be. Snake is the eternal creator of all. Snake created NO Dom, sets all plans in motion, and gives all direction. Snake gives laws and ordinances. Snake supplies everything needed for life, like food, clothing, and shelter. Snake provides for your well-being and health. Snake supplies all employment. Snake is in full control of everyone's lives. Snake is intelligent and all-wise, full of integrity, truth, and honesty. Snake is love and

compassion. Snake is eloquent in appearance. He sees all and knows all. Yes, Snake, Dragon of Old, the Powerful Darkness, has a driving desire to see the best for everyone. No one is greater or wiser.

"This gives you authority and power over everyone," Cur'sent noted. "We'll train our troops to doubt Olam. As for the Claydoms, they are little more than cannon fodder."

Snake nodded. "You're realizing who I am and what I'm capable of."

"Snake, I give my life to you," Cardinal said, kneeling down before him. "We will eliminate Olam and make you the mightiest and most powerful god."

Cur'sent knelt beside her and made the same pledge.

"Olam said that these Claydoms are like us, spirit and also physical." Cur'sent blinked in confusion. "I'm not sure what that means. But if they're like us, they'll do anything to protect themselves. And in protecting themselves, they'll do anything and be easily distracted from Olam."

Life's Struggle

Not long after the Claydoms moved, their first beautiful baby was born into the family. Then came the finishing of a new lodge, finding new sources of food, making clothing, providing water, and gathering wood to keep them warm and cook.

Over the course of years, Kindle and Twilight had many children, and their children had children as well. Soon they had both grandchildren and great-grandchildren as well.

One day, the couple reminisced about their lives so far. Although they were happy, they wished that their nature wasn't so demanding.

"I know that Snake's forces are around us," Kindle remarked. "Like Chief Olam said, though, we made our choice. We have to accept responsibility for it and not blame our disobedience on others. We are the cause of what's happened."

As the number of Claydoms increased, many heard the story of the very beginning, what had happened when Kindle and Twilight had disobeyed Olam.

The uncomfortable truth for Snake and his forces was that the Claydoms also excelled at doing good in the world. Many of them still connected with Olam and helped others. Whenever

Snake heard of a Claydom doing good, he could be heard for hours ranting and bellowing in resentment.

"Kill them all. Get rid of those doing good! I hate them."

As the disobedient were killed or died, Snake gloated.

"They're mine," he would insist with flashing eyes. "They're all mine!"

As Kindle and Twilight grew older, they gazed over their paradise.

"Our beautiful valley has been well used," said Kindle. "I sometimes wonder what it would've been like if we hadn't picked that flower."

"I wonder as well, but we can't change the past," his wife replied. "It is what it is. What troubles me most right now is the selfishness in our family."

"It bothers me as well," said Kindle.

Twilight grew silent as she realized that her own disobedience had brought her and her family to this situation.

She took Kindle's hand as a tear trickled down her husband's cheek. They cried together, unable to change what they'd chosen.

Watching their vulnerability, Olam's tears fell, too. Although the couple couldn't see him, he stood silently by their sides, preventing Snake's forces from destroying them.

Once their emotions were under control again, Olam decided to allow them to perceive him.

"Chief Olam!" Kindle said. "I apologize for not trusting you. I'm sorry for my disobedience. I became very selfish, and everything that happened afterward has been so very wrong. I'm deeply sorry for my choice."

"I'm pleased to accept your apology," said Olam. "I forgive you for your disobedience."

As Kindle heard Olam's words, an immense peace filled him.

Twilight also expressed her regret and apologized for her disobedience. In the same way that Olam had forgiven Kindle, he forgave her.

"But out of immense respect for you, and because you chose the life you have, I can't change your decision," Olam told them. "Live in peace, forgiven. I love you each very much."

The Claydoms returned to their lodge that evening, full of appreciation for Olam's forgiveness. They knew now that Olam waited in the shadows, watching over them even when they couldn't see him.

Being physical, life eventually caught up to Kindle and Twilight. Their kids grew, married, and had kids and grandkids who moved to still other parts of Claydonia. But the first couple remained living in their beloved valley. Whenever asked, they told their story of being forgiven. They spoke often of the peace they enjoyed. They also chatted with Olam many times.

One night, Kindle tenderly held Twilight as she breathed her last.

The following day, Kindle and the local members of the family buried her in their beloved valley.

A few mornings later, when Kindle didn't emerge from his lodge, his children found him in the very same spot where Twilight had laid when she passed away. They buried him beside his beloved wife.

Snake's Plan

As the family expanded outward, so too did the dense cloud that had originally come from the east. It now loomed heavy over Claydonia. Amidst this darkness, with the support of Ly'Bar, Shrew, and Acc'Plish, the Claydoms tamed animals for labour, food, and clothing. Spices, minerals, gold, silver, and jewelled ornaments were traded. Tin, iron, and copper were mined, smelted, manufactured, and shipped. Oil and tar were transported over rivers, lakes, and oceans. Beer, wine, drugs, and narcotics were harvested and traded.

The Claydoms built cities. As their economies flourished, they formed governments bent on the dark curse of self-fulfillment. They built armies to protect themselves, to war over, and to control. It seemed there was nothing the Claydoms could not do and Snake's image was displayed in every nation, language, and creed.

From the stories of Kindle and Twilight, many understood Chief Olam and spoke to him. And when they did, he forgave them.

Over time, some Claydoms organized into groups to talk and learn about Olam. They built structures to meet in and formed religious organizations. Once these structures were finished, though, the people forgot why they had built them and spent time caring for them instead of the Claydoms in need. Many priests were nothing more than thieves and rogues. The Claydoms flaunted their connection to religion. And the Claydoms didn't only form religions dedicated to Olam; they also formed others for Snake.

Yet many talked with Olam about Dominion and becoming spirit-oriented.

Million died as the population increased, due to disease, drought, famine, floods, earthquakes, and calamitous storms. The Claydoms did everything to save themselves, with Snake's encouragement. As they focused on their physical selves, Claydonia grew even darker.

As the Claydoms' physical life developed, they became more captive to their physical orientation. This selfish, controlling, independent dissension dragged the Claydoms deeper into the oozing darkness from the east.

Olam came and asked the Claydoms to lead peaceful lives, but the curse of disobedience prevailed. The more Olam tried to help, the more the Claydoms shifted towards anarchy. Their rebellious nature was so great that many were destroyed under its massive weight.

The skies over the land became so dark that the Claydoms began to prefer it to light.

In this darkness, Snake continued his efforts to gather a massive army of Claydoms to fight back against Olam.

One day, Snake called his top commanders to his office.

"Cardinal, how's our propaganda going?" he asked. "We need to get the Claydoms to believe everything is all about themselves. To promote this selfishness, let's get the Claydoms to refer to themselves as I and me."

"Yes Snake, that's good, so far it's working well. When their selfishness kicks in, they divide into small groups and demand to get their own way instead of uniting. I think they feel more secure in these small groups. When they feel small, they seek to soothe their addiction to self."

Cur'sent agreed with this. "I'm taken aback by the length a Claydom will go to as the badly treated underdog. The more abused they get, the more vulnerable, the greater they feel themselves to be. They demand their rights with extreme authority and control."

"Good observations!" Snake said. "The longer they remain in these small ethnic groups, the more we can keep them embroiled in petty disagreements. It's all 'us versus them.' They'll march in the streets and demand their rights and smash things up."

"Dissension, bigotry, racism, and discrimination is on the rise," Cardinal added. "There's a real sense that a kind of madness is getting out of control. Eventually there'll be no Claydoms left."

Snake smiled at this. "We're trying to bring about the breakdown of their society. To promote this, parents must turn against their kids, and kids against their parents. That way, the kids are mine to play with. They're mine for life. I'll groom them for my own pleasure, exercising full control over them. Soon I'll form a single Claydonian government and demand that the leaders dumb the people down so they'll not be able to reason for themselves. Then I can do whatever I want with them. I will decide who gets fed, who gets housing and clothes and medical care. I decide who lives and who doesn't. If the Claydoms are fully obedient to me, life will be good. If not, I'll kill them."

Insults

Chief Olam shook his head, knowing that a massive devastation would soon consume the Claydoms. He gathered his generals to discuss the situation.

"You know that I hold you all and the Claydoms in high esteem," he opened.

"Chief, I heard you tell Kindle and Twilight that they're of immense value to you," Cha'el said. "You also told them that you love them. And I know you love all of Dominion the same. And yet you're troubled about the Claydoms. How's your plan coming for them?"

"I don't like what I see, but it's their choice," Olam acknowledged. "I must leave them to their will. It won't be much longer. For now, we'll let O'bed and In'Mutin work things out."

At their headquarters in Claydonia, Cur'sent and Cardinal retired to the conference room with In'Mutin in tow. They intended to fill in their special agent on important developments.

"The authorities, leaders, and scientists of the Claydoms consider themselves providers. They proclaim themselves to supply good health, housing, clothing, and food, ensuring that the Claydoms are employed and financially secure. They say, 'We have the wisdom and ability to care for you! Trust us!' Do you know anything about this, In'Mutin?"

In'Mutin smiled. "If you must know, that's my work!"

"In'Mutin, you're bragging," said Cur'sent with a frown.

"Yea, I am. And why shouldn't I? The Claydoms are bent on disobedience." In'Mutin looked from one to the other. "You know, I'm loyal to Snake. He may not be able to walk, but he's still Supreme and Wise Ruler of NO Dom."

Cur'sent was viciously angry and about to say so, but Cardinal put her hand on his shoulder to stop him from standing.

"These Claydoms are deplorables," In'Mutin said. "They'll be very useful when deployed as a force against Olam. And you two need to hear me, and hear me well: I'm a major player in this war. Neither of you will hinder me in my assignment. If you want to help, I'll allow it, but step carefully."

With that, In'Mutin walked out and slammed the door shut behind him.

Cur'sent smacked his hands down onto the tabletop, glaring at the door. He sat brooding in silence for several minutes.

"You know, Cur'sent, we're still in charge," Cardinal reminded him. "Even if he doesn't acknowledge it."

"I hate him. Who does he think he is coming in here and insulting me?"

From Snake's viewpoint, the waterfalls were shrouded in a thick haze. And to the north, there was a source of brightness… something he had never seen before in that part of Claydonia.

He called out for Cur'sent and Cardinal to come into his office and see the phenomenon for themselves, but by the time they arrived the brightness was fading. The waterfalls had fallen back into darkness.

A vast insecurity ruffled Snake's confidence. Were they still in control of this war?

As the acquaintances diminished in influence, the Claydoms came to trust their own authorities. To further destabilize the situation, Snake sent out Tum and Bed to terrorize them. Tum poked and jeered the Claydoms, causing them to fear anything and everything. Then, as storms and floods swept in and threatened the Claydoms, Bed produced as much hopelessness as he could, leaving the Claydoms in despair.

To facilitate Snake's hatred of Olam and his forces, Snake declared all good Claydoms as his sworn opposition and enemy. He even ordered Cur'sent to address the troops, hammering on the podium and shouting, "All Claydoms who aren't for Snake are our enemy!"

The troops cheered. "Stomp 'em! Our enemy! Stomp 'em! Kill 'em! Filthy pig! Sticking sewer rats!"

"They're enemies of Snake, Dragon of Old, the Powerful Darkness!" Cur'sent shouted, egging them on.

"Snake! Snake! Mighty Snake! Snake, our great god!"

In this way, Snake claimed authority over all the tribes and nations of Claydoms, demanding they worship him as Supreme and Wise Ruler. This led to the destruction of every Claydom not part of NO Dom. Snake was prevailing.

JAILED

Ever since first bringing Kindle and Twilight to Claydonia, Olam had allowed every Claydom to either sign up with him or Snake. As the war had gained momentum, though, the years proved that these disobedient Claydoms did fortify Snake's forces. With these additions to his troops, Snake believed he could eliminate Olam.

But as this played out in Claydonia, Olam continued with his original plan.

"Generals, it's time that the Claydoms have my direct input to bring the plan to a successful conclusion," he declared when he gathered his leaders for a meeting. "I will step into the physical myself to be like the Claydoms. Once they see and hear me, hopefully they can know what it means to be spirit-oriented."

When Snake heard that Olam was coming to Claydonia, his anger predictably exploded. In his rage, he immediately left Claydonia himself, intent on traveling to Dominion to kill the commander-in-chief before he could carry out his plan.

Seeing Snake coming, Olam sent his generals to arrest the rebel.

Before long, Snake was cowering before Olam at the First Division headquarters.

"Snake, you were instructed not to leave Claydonia unless I called you," Olam pronounced. "You've been defiant and left Claydonia. As directed, I must now imprison you." He nodded to his generals. "Throw him into the dungeon that's been prepared for him."

As soon as they saw Snake leave headquarters, Cur'sent and Cardinal had raced after him, to stop him from making a big mistake. When they saw him get captured by Olam and the generals of Dominion, they quickly returned to Claydonia.

They were on hand to watch as Olam's generals deposited Snake in his new dungeon in the dark, arid wasteland southeast of NO Dom headquarters. As they approached the gate, they could already hear Snake's voice cursing Olam.

"Snake!" Cur'sent called in. "Snake, we're here!"

Snake slithered to the gate and looked out. "Get me out of here—now!"

But Cur'sent and Cardinal searched every side of the dungeon, looking for any weakness, and were unable to find a way out.

"Olam, you filthy, good for nothing pig… you stinking sewer rat," Snake hissed and yelled, stewing in his cage. "I'll kill you!"

"Snake, settle down or we're leaving," Cur'sent demanded.

This stopped Snake cold. Simpering, he returned to the gate.

"What do you want us to do now?" Cardinal asked.

Snake cleared his throat. "Here's what you're going to do. Cur'sent, you'll represent me."

"Yes, sir!"

"Wear my crown. With my powers and authority, I need you to lead my forces and gather as many Claydoms as possible. Those who refuse to come to NO Dom are to be considered deplorables. Kill them! Do you hear me?"

"Yes, sir. Your command is my obedience."

"Good! As for you, Cardinal, you're now second in command! You also have all the power and authority to execute what I've ordered Cur'sent to do. Do the same. Do you hear me?"

"Yes, sir!"

Both Cur'sent and Cardinal snapped to attention.

"Keep me informed." He retreated from the bars, mumbling to himself in a mocking tone. "I'll relish controlling these appalling Claydoms or destroying them. Either way, Olam can't have them…"

At headquarters, Cur'sent and Cardinal called their generals. Before going into the conference room, Cur'sent placed Snake's crown upon his own head, as ordered, and as he did this Snake's vile nature filled him and Cardinal completely. That defiant ego came oozing out of them. They stood in awe of this power.

"Cardinal, I say that we present ourselves as two," said Cur'sent. "But in reality, we're one in nature, so interwoven that we cannot exist without each other."

When Cur'sent took off the crown, though, he realized that the immense power went with it. The power was tied to the crown.

He put the crown back on.

"Generals," Cur'sent declared upon entering the conference room. "Olam has abducted Snake. He's being abused and imprisoned against his will."

"Then we'll go and get him out," Zez demanded.

Cardinal sighed. "The dungeon is highly secure. There's no way to release him."

"Snake has put me in command and positioned Cardinal as my second in command until further notice," Cur'sent explained. "Snake has demanded that we gather all the Claydoms we can to push us to victory over Olam. Dismissed!"

A Physical Life

With Snake locked up, Olam finally carried out his plan by stepping out of the spirit world and entering the physical. Physically entering Claydonia was challenging and came with many strange sensations.

Over time, as he walked, talked, and lived among the Claydoms, they began to trust him. Wherever he went, crowds listened. They watched how he challenged the authorities and defended those who were treated unjustly.

Many asked, "Would you teach us how to live as a spirit?"

He showed them how to live free of the physical curse and be aware of their selfish and disobedient natures.

"You're free to choose and live as you want," Olam said. "You don't have to be held captive by the physical curse. My acquaintances will help you live your lives."

But Olam had a destabilizing influence on Claydom society. As more and more people grew to become spirit-oriented, the authorities grew more desperate to kill Olam before they completely lost control. From their perspective, Olam was destroying their very way of life.

Not having anticipated his coming, Cur'sent and Cardinal froze when they heard that Olam himself was walking amongst the Claydoms.

"Cardinal, what do you think he's up to?" Cur'sent asked one day from Snake's office.

Feeling defensive, Cardinal leaned back in her seat. "I don't know. I have no idea whatsoever! Why now?"

As usual, their answer was to scramble together a meeting of the generals. Within a few hours, everyone was gathered in the conference room.

"You should have given us a heads up about this business about Olam showing up in person," Zez demanded.

Cur'sent spat angrily. "We just found out! Where's your surveillance, Zez? Why didn't your forces pick up on something?"

"He doesn't even look like himself," Cardinal said. "He's here in the same physical form as the Claydoms. He looks like them. We need to get our surveillance on him right now and find out what's going on."

The generals hurried out, leaving the top brass to stew.

That day, In'Mutin rushed into Cardinal's office, demanding to know what was going on. Cardinal stood, stepped around her desk, and then led him out to meet Cur'sent.

Cur'sent looked up in surprise when they entered. "What's up?"

"I need to know—" In'Mutin growled.

"Shut up and listen," Cur'sent interrupted. "We don't know! Don't come in here demanding things. Do you hear me?"

In'Mutin was taken aback. "All right…"

"I should throw you out of here right now—"

But Cardinal stepped in. "We're just getting reports now on what Olam has been up to. It looks like the Claydom authorities are so upset that they're going to kill him."

"What's he done?" In'Mutin asked.

"If you're so smart, shouldn't you already know?" Cur'sent glared at him. "He's getting the Claydoms to choose the spirit life over physical life. I thought you were supposed to be looking after this, In'Mutin. Why didn't you stop this from getting so far?"

In'Mutin replied in a smooth, mocking tone. "Settle down, Cur'sent. I've got this—"

Cur'sent jumped to his feet and slapped his desk. "You're the biggest liar there is. You don't have it! And don't tell me you do. If you were doing your job, Olam wouldn't be convincing the Claydoms to become spirit-oriented."

"But how much more is there than the physical life of a Claydom?" In'Mutin taunted. "Besides, if the authorities hate Olam as much as we do, the problem will take care of itself. And when they kill him, Dominion won't have a chief anymore. And then all of Dominion will be ours. All ours!"

In'Mutin leaned smugly over Cur'sent's desk.

"Don't you see, Cur'sent?" the agent jeered. "It's best to just let the Claydoms do the dirty work for us."

Cardinal thought about this. "Yes. Then the Claydoms will liberate themselves from his power, control, demands, and so-called freedom. In liberating themselves, they'll liberate us. Being liberated, we'll liberate Snake. Then we can liberate Dominion for ourselves."

"Okay," Cur'sent said, calming down. "I'd say your job, In'Mutin, is to make sure your influence on the Claydoms is compelling. Compelling enough for them to carry through with their intentions to kill Olam. And if you don't do it, I'll personally make sure you're finished. Got it?"

In'Mutin glared at him. "Sure, boss."

The agent left the office, smiling to himself while gloating over poking his boss.

Them vs. Us

Olam continued to do his best for others, helping the Claydoms by instructing them in the spirit life and the ways of Dominion. Meanwhile, the authorities kept declaring him a fraud, calling him a filthy pig and stinking sewer rat, an illiterate, uneducated, ignorant Neanderthal who lacked moral authority. To many, he was known as a toxic Claydom.

Not only did the authorities discredit Olam, but they mistreated those who joined Dominion. They even killed Olam's followers. Many Claydoms chose not to associate with Olam out of fear of the authorities, ignoring their families and friends who were spirit-oriented.

The authorities launched brutally attacks on Olam, and the physically-oriented Claydoms took these attacks as permission to do the same. All sorts of scoundrels supported the scheme to eliminate Olam for good.

Eventually they brutally murdered him, thinking they were finally rid of him and in complete control of Claydonia.

Upon discovering that Olam had been murdered, a mighty force of Claydoms arose to place his body in a coffin.

Three days later, they came together and held a funeral—only they discovered that he had somehow left the coffin.

Later that day, Olam appeared to many of his followers and assured them that he would be as he had been before. He encouraged them to be strong, courageous, and spirit-oriented.

"I will wait for you when you leave your physical forms," he said. "I will return to liberate Claydonia from this darkness."

Cur'sent and Cardinal soon received an important dispatch from General Abb: "Olam is returning to liberate Claydonia." Upon hearing this, they felt that their dream of taking Dominion for themselves was melting away.

"I was convinced that we had power over the Claydoms," Cur'sent pondered. "But I'm seeing now that we don't. I can't believe so many thousands would still join Olam, even after his killing. I thought we'd have full control over them... but no."

"The authorities didn't know what they were doing, it turns out," Cardinal agreed. "When they killed him, all they did was release him from the physical."

A solemn silence fell over the pair.

"We've been fighting Olam's freedom all our lives." Cardinal put her head in her hands. "According to Olam, we've made a choice. These Claydoms, though, are choosing to be spirit-oriented. So when they die their physical deaths, they're liberated to be with Olam. Yet we have those who choose a physical orientation. It has to be one or the other."

Cur'sent nodded. "We only have one more chance to get this right. Let's get as many Claydoms on our side as possible to take on Olam. By winning, we can finally liberate ourselves from him."

"The Claydoms will have to focus on their physical life. If they choose to be spirit-oriented, we'll have to destroy them."

"Olam thinks he's going to win. But if we launch a strong retaliation, I still think we can take him. We just have to prevent the Claydoms from finding out that they can escape Snake's control. We'll make them so afraid that they won't want to choose the spirit life."

Wearing the crown, Cur'sent went down to the conference room.

"If we're going to get ourselves out of the situation we're in, we must launch a counterattack," he announced when he sat down in front of the generals. "Olam thinks he's got us, but in actuality we've got him."

Cardinal nodded. "We need a plan to emphasize to the Claydoms that it's either them or us."

"If the Claydoms are mixed, though, how will we know who's on which side?" asked Zez.

"We'll mark our own," In'Mutin said.

"Wouldn't it be easier to mark the ones who are with Olam?" Abb wondered. "There won't be many of them."

Cardinal rubbed her tired eyes. "Either way, how will we mark them? They're so independent."

"We'll make them do it," said Cur'sent. "We'll eliminate them otherwise. As long as they're scared, they'll do anything we want them to do."

Brutus seemed skeptical. "Just because we mark them, that doesn't mean we control them."

"No," agreed Zez. "But as we've seen, it makes them feel more like the animals we see them as."

"So we just need the Claydom authorities to implement the marking system," Caridnal said.

In'Mutin brightened up. "That's my job! And it's an easy one."

Cur'sent ignored the agent. "Okay, we all know our jobs. We have to make sure everyone knows it's us versus them. And they'll only live if they join us."

The meeting broke up and Cur'sent and Cardinal walked out of the conference room, heading back to Cur'sent's office.

"Do you really think this will work?" Cardinal asked.

"Yes, absolutely."

"Why?"

"Because I've done this all my life, and I always get what I want. You know that. My main concern is whether the Claydom authorities can pull it off."

"I'm quite sure they can. They've taken after Snake by now. Besides, didn't they already show us by killing Olam?"

Cur'sent smiled. "Yes! That was a real surprise. When I think about it, it's like In'Mutin says: leave it to them, and they'll do the dirty work for us."

It turned out to be easy to encourage the authorities to start separating the Claydoms into two camps, them and us. It wasn't long before the spirit-oriented Claydoms were complaining about being mistreated, picked on, ridiculed, and left out. The unrest spread like wildfire across Claydonia.

Desperation

Many Claydoms rebelled against their authorities and the push to take away their freedom to choose—to speak freely and do what they wanted, where they wanted, when they wanted. And to accelerate the genocide, the authorities confiscated all Claydom property while disarming them so they had nothing to support or defend themselves with. Millions were eliminated as filthy pigs and toxic, sewer rats. The lists of these deplorables were circulated; those who knew someone on the list could do whatever they wanted to them. Nothing would be said or done.

All the while, the more pressure the authorities exerted, the more Claydoms found themselves drawn to Olam. The spirit-oriented Claydoms fed the hungry and dug wells to supply water to the thirsty. They collected clothing and supplies for those without. They shipped medical and school supplies and equipment to those who needed it. During emergencies, they provided aid. Where there were wars, the spirit-oriented helped the refugees and wounded. Amidst terrorist bombings and killings, they risked their lives to help those suffering. They appealed to the governments of Claydonia to stop the bloodshed. They spoke up against injustice in the midst of civil unrest. They followed the way of Dominion, choose to do the best for others, no matter the cost.

During this time, Olam at last released Snake from prison, returning him to his original form. This gave Snake time to prepare for the final battle.

Olam wanted Snake to lead the enemy forces, so that he wouldn't be able to later claim that it had been an unfair battle. It was going to be a fair fight and the losers would know they had been defeated. It would also give the winner the right to judge and sentence the loser to their final punishment.

In preparation for the final battle, Snake called a war council. The conference room soon filled up with all his top supporters. They were feeling desperate.

"Thank you for your support," Snake began. "Olam is amassing a huge force. If we want to save ourselves, we must counter it, no matter what. We're now in an all-out campaign to gather as many Claydoms as possible. I demand total genocide of all the filthy pigs and stinking sewer rats who associate with Olam. We must prepare for a battle like none we've ever seen before." He turned to his right. "Cur'sent, what are your thoughts?"

"Snake, we're all glad you're back," Cur'sent replied. "First, we must deny the consequences of all our actions against the Claydoms. This will make them focus on Olam and blame him. If we take credit, we'll only drive more Claydoms to Olam."

Snake smiled. "Brilliant, Cur'sent! What's your take, Cardinal?"

"He's correct," she said. "We must enforce this amongst our troops. The Claydoms must blame Olam for everything."

As this settled in, Zez spoke up. "The faster we eliminate the spirit-oriented Claydoms, the better it'll be for us. We must end their influence so that the remaining Claydoms can be convinced to choose our side."

Satisfied, Snake dismissed his upper brass and returned to his office. From the window, he looked down on the parade square. There was a flurry of activity below as each general assembled the troops to outfit them for the coming battle.

As the situation in Claydonia intensified, Olam and his forces continued to encourage the Claydoms to search for truth in everything they did, confident that when a Claydom discovered the truth it would set them free from the captivity of their physical lives.

Olam also watched the armament of Snake's forces and kept his eye on the brutal exterminations throughout the lands. Many Claydoms refused to follow Snake's demands, despite the consequences.

Times were extremely difficult. Soon the authorities didn't only seek to kill the spirit-oriented; they also chose to kill the undecided. To them, it was better to die than be free to choose Olam.

Final Battle

When Cur'sent and Cardinal received a dispatch reporting that Olam had begun to form up his troops for the last battle, they rushed into Snake's office.

"Snake!" Cur'sent called. "Olam has ordered his troops to gather here in Claydonia."

Snake stood up. "Order our generals to prepare for immediate action."

Within days, both armies were assembled against each other on the battlefield, the largest Claydonia had ever hosted in its long history.

On one side, Olam stood at the forefront, looking out over the enemy.

"Position yourselves and await orders to bring over the Claydom who wish to join us," Olam declared to the member of a special joint taskforce. "As for the rest of you, wait for my signal to engage our enemy."

On the other side, Snake surveyed alongside his commanding officers.

"Brute, when I lift my weapon, that will be the signals for you to begin eliminating all Claydoms in sight, no matter their orientation," he ordered. Brutus beamed with excitement, ready to execute his driving desire to eliminate anyone and everything.

If Brutus was surprised by this sudden change in strategy, he didn't show it.

"First and Second Divisions, it will be your responsibility to prevent Olam's forces from advancing," Snake continued. "They must not stop this genocide."

Before the battle could begin in earnest, however, it was Olam who stepped forward first—not to fight, but rather to call Snake to meet.

As the two met in the middle of the battlefield, Olam's forces got to work gathering all who were spirit-oriented, bringing them over to Dominion's side.

"It's with great regret that we've come to this point," Olam said to his enemy. "There's still time to prevent the carnage that is about to take place. It's your choice."

Snake angrily shook his fists in defiance. "You've stolen from me my rightful place as commander-in-chief of Dominion. You've cheated me out of the rewards for all my accomplishments. You've lied to me, my forces, and Claydonia, insisting that your way is better. No, Olam! This is the deciding moment. The bloodshed will be on your head, and you'll pay greatly for it."

With this declaration, Snake drew his sword.

At this signal, Brutus issued a command for his division to begin the slaughter of all Claydoms. These killings were carried out with such savagery that blood ran through the fields like a mighty river.

Meanwhile, Olam held his battle lines secure, still waiting for all spirit-oriented Claydoms to join his forces.

Snake broke into laughter, with his great genocide well underway.

"Olam!" he taunted. "Your precious Claydoms are gone forever. And so will you."

At last Olam gave the signal. His troops burst forward, surging over Snake and his forces as if they were nothing but toys of Claydom children.

Punishment

With the battle lost, Snake stood in the revealing light of the new dawn, looking out over the carnage. In bewilderment, he removed his crown and gazed around him. Cur'sent, Cardinal, In'Mutin, and the generals of his army lay dead at his feet where they had defended him to their last. Their bodies were silent, weapons held in their limp hands. Their voices would never again be heard.

Watching Snake, Olam raised his hand and signaled for the fighting to cease. All became quiet as the darkness over Snake's forces dissipated, replaced by brilliant light.

Olam then signaled for his generals to gather all those enemy forces who remained standing and lead them to wait for judgement alongside Snake, their commander-in-chief.

When Olam at last approached them, he looked his former enemy in the eyes.

"Cypher, you claimed to be the Supreme and Wise Ruler of your NO Dominion. You called yourself Snake, Dragon of Old, the Powerful Darkness. You were correct in that you're the father of all liars. The patriarch of the selfish and egocentric. The author who promotes lying, stealing, and cheating.

The pitch-black darkness of the east. The source of all disobedience. You, Cypher, who is so conceited, could not see yourself and would not change who you are. You claimed to be light but could not overcome the Light. As a general, you rebelled against me, Dominion, and all that Dominion stands for. Now look upon your achievements. Your so-called glory has spread across Claydonia. Cypher! You chose to be disobedient, and now you stand amidst the result of that choice."

Olam looked down upon the bodies of Snake's greatest commanders.

"Behold Cur'sent, the selfish curse sent upon all who are disobedient. He now lies defeated at your feet, stripped of all power and authority. Behold Cardinal, the one with the persuasive power to mislead and twist the truth. She has been silenced forever. Behold In'Mutin! The insubordinate one who in mutiny fulfills all his selfish desires. Behold Zez, the mother of all who are like Jezebel, the ruthless woman who controlled and murdered the ones sent to help the Claydoms achieve a better life. She represents all who are enslaved by their vile, selfish ways. Behold Abb, who represents all vile traitors who plotted to kill my Claydoms and, as Ahab did, plundered their lives and property. Behold Brutus, who represents the brutality that brought an end to so many."

Silence settled over the broken landscape.

"Cypher, you tried stopping me from bringing the Claydoms to the place I prepared for them," Olam continued. "I also prepared that place for you. And yet you ravaged Claydonia, leaving it a desolate wasteland. You then chose to fight this last battle to satisfy your ego. In your self-centred ways, you could not see how it would end, because you despised me. Now you've become the despised."

Snake looked down at the ground, awaiting his sentence.

"Cypher, I have always done what is best for others. I will not, and cannot, do anything else. And so I will not leave you in eternal turmoil."

Olam raised his hand and then brought it down swiftly. With this final signal, all who remained of Snake's forces were executed.

Snake now stood alone, revealed in Olam's light.

Dominion's commander-in-chief made direct eye contact with the counterfeit. "Cypher, it's with great pain and sadness that I now carry out the results of your choice."

With this, Olam took from Snake his sword and quickly executed him. His enemy's crown tumbled to the ground, landing in a puddle of splattered Claydom blood.

Going Home

Once Adon Olam had executed his final duty as commander-in-chief of Dominion, he, his troops, and the liberated left Claydonia and set out again to return to Dominion.

They spared a moment to look back. Alongside Olam stood Cha'el, Stren, Rafal, and Barac. Behind them, the army of the liberated stood in watchful silence, observing their commander-in-chief and his generals. Together, they paused and thought of the events that had transpired.

Once Olam had paid tribute to his beloved Claydoms, he looked to his generals.

"It's been a hard trial for me to watch today's events," he said. "But now I must destroy Claydonia for good, so that the memories of disobedience the land represents doesn't come back to haunt us."

After he spoke, a great fire arose and consumed Claydonia, leaving nothing of the once beautiful and sprawling country. Everything perished in this all-consuming fire.

"Let's take our forces and return home. We have great and exciting times ahead of us. Let's go!"

Never again did Olam speak of Claydonia, nor the Claydoms who had rejected him and passed away. Instead he rejoiced and celebrated all who had come to him. They lived together in Dominion, enjoying its greatness—and as always, doing the best for each other.

Again, a beautiful golden sunrise broke in the east as Chief Adon Olam, strolled peacefully beside the river that wound its way through the majestic parklands. Along the way, he paused to smell flowers, listen to birds, and watch wildlife. As the day warmed, a slight breeze teased the grass and rustled the dew-laden trees, causing droplets of water to fall to the moss-covered earth.

About the Author

Tim Kirby was born in Drumheller, Alberta. The second of five children, he is the son of a Second World War veteran and Saskatchewan maiden. He graduated from high school in hard times and then attended university. Afterward he held many positions from Winnipeg to Vancouver Island and served as a hospital and Royal Canadian Legion chaplain. He's an avid writer and photographer. He is married to his wife Sharron, and together they have three grown sons and their families.

His outlook on life is simple: there's nothing we can't do, but there are things we shouldn't do! And also, truth and justice are paramount and vital for living.

He is the author of *The Green Soother*, a tribal look at words and their meaning. For example, the tribal word for "love" means to do the best for another, no matter the cost. He also authored *Last Moments*, a book of stories of real people who loved, toiled, and for various reasons suffered from disease, accidents, war, and old age. With each story, he remembers how they impacted his life and became part of who he is. He has also written many poems that have been accepted with gratitude and warm compliments.